Ivy Takes Care

★

Ivy Takes Care

ROSEMARY WELLS

illustrations by Jim LaMarche

CANDLEWICK PRESS

Text copyright © 2013 by Rosemary Wells
Illustrations copyright © 2013 by Jim LaMarche

Photograph on page 200 courtesy of the author

First paperback edition 2015

Library of Congress Catalog Card Number 2012942383
ISBN 978-0-7636-5352-1 (hardcover)
ISBN 978-0-7636-7660-5 (paperback)

14 15 16 17 18 19 BVG 10 9 8 7 6 5 4 3 2 1

Printed in Berryville, VA, U.S.A.

This book was typeset in Bembo.
The illustrations were done using acrylic washes
and pencils on watercolor paper.

Candlewick Press
99 Dover Street
Somerville, Massachusetts 02144

visit us at www.candlewick.com

For Mrs. Bowers

R. W.

Chestnut

Ivy willed her legs to be like pistons. She pedaled her way up Canyon Road, sweating and pushing her muscles to overcome the steep upward grade. In her fifth-grade science book, gleaming steel pistons were pictured under the heading "How an Engine Works," but the pistons in the textbook engine felt no pain. Ivy's legs and lungs burned with the effort of the uphill ride. Later, she thought, *If I'd been going along at twenty miles an hour, I never would have seen the turtle, and who knows how things would have worked out?*

It lay on its back, still alive but having been hit by a car, covered with blood and road dirt. It was a big desert tortoise. Ivy righted it gently and examined the wound. "Nasty!" said Ivy. "But fixable. I'm going to have to take you up to Annie's house and hose you off," said Ivy. "Give you some water and let you rest. And maybe you'd like a raw egg to eat."

Annie wouldn't mind her bringing the turtle. Annie understood Ivy better than anyone in the world, and had since they had both been five. And Annie's mother wouldn't mind the filthy turtle nearly so much as Ivy's own mother would.

Cheerfully, then, Ivy wedged the bleeding turtle into her bicycle basket and pumped the heavily laden bike up the next ten switchbacks to Canyon Ridge. Straddling Canyon Ridge, the mansions of the old silver-mining families looked out over western Nevada, valley on one side, the Washoe mountains on the other.

That Saturday afternoon's visit to Annie was to be a good-bye visit. Annie was headed, the next day, two thousand miles away to summer camp in New Hampshire. For the last two summers, Annie went east in June, a few days after school was over, and stayed until just before Labor Day, when school began again. Annie's mother and grandmother had all gone to Camp Allegro on Silver Lake when they were girls.

Allegro had its own mystique. Even though Annie had taught Ivy to sing every one of the Camp Allegro songs, the white-and-green–outfitted girls remained a puzzlement to Ivy. Annie did not explain the mystery because none of it was part of Ivy's world or ever would be.

Ivy pulled into Annie's driveway, crunching the gravel as she did. Annie's mother stood with a hose, watering the delicate Russian sage and the small balloons of scarlet mallow that filled her garden. She raised a hand in greeting and smiled. "What have you got there, Ivy?" she called across the garden.

"A turtle, Mrs. Evans," Ivy answered, lifting the injured creature, whose head and legs had retreated inside its shell, "He's hurt. Can I use the hose to clean him off, please?"

"Of course," said Annie's mother. "Bring him over. Put him down right here. Poor thing. Hit by a car?"

"Yep, I think so, probably," said Ivy. She ran the cold water over the dirty shell and gently into the wound, clearing it of gravel and sand. "What I could use," said Ivy, now kneeling in the soft grass by the side of her patient, "is some duct tape."

"Duct tape?" asked Annie's mother.

"Duct tape will hold anything together pretty permanently and protect the wound. I figure if he lives and the shell grows back, the duct tape'll

4

just be shed off. I hope maybe if I put him in the woodshed and give him an egg, he might eat it."

"Egg?" asked Annie's mother.

"Raw egg. It's in *The Home Vet*," explained Ivy. Ivy had studied up about what lots of creatures ate in the one book her father owned, *The Home Veterinarian*. Not that Ivy's dad was an actual vet. He was stableman at the Red Star Ranch and he just looked up horse ailments.

"Good idea!" said Annie's mother. Ivy adored Annie's mother. She didn't like to think she loved her more than her own mom, but Ivy's mother worked so hard and got so bone tired every night after all the dishes were put away and the ranch kitchen cleaned for breakfast, she had no time to be easy-breezy like Annie's mother. Annie's mother got to water her flower garden and do good deeds all day if she wanted.

"Leave the turtle inside the petunia bed,

honey. He can't get out. Come in the kitchen way," said Annie's mother. "We'll get an egg and maybe some celery for that poor creature. Let me get you a new shirt. That one's covered in turtle blood. Annie has a friend from camp here for the night."

"Friend?" asked Ivy. Ivy had never met anyone else in the world who went to Camp Allegro. Ivy didn't want that friend, whoever she was, to be there and interrupt her and Annie's last afternoon together before the Annie-empty eleven-week summer set in. The friend made Camp Allegro more real than Ivy wanted it to be. They entered the kitchen. Annie's mother rested a bunch of her garden flowers on the counter.

"A California girl," said Annie's mother, removing an egg from the fridge and rustling in a drawer for the tape. "Annie!" she called out toward the porch. "Did you take that roll of silver tape we had in here?"

A muffled *"What?"* came from the porch five rooms away.

"I said, did you take that big roll of silvery tape out of the kitchen drawer for some reason?" her mother repeated loudly.

This question was not answered. Annie in person came into the kitchen with two empty glasses in her hand. "What, Mom?" she said.

"Not *What, Mom.* Say, *I can't hear you, Mom,*" corrected her mother. "Where's that silver tape in the big fat roll, honey?"

Annie was followed by another girl, with tawny eyes and stylishly bobbed hair, sleek as a mink.

"Hey! Ive!" said Annie, "Meet my tent mate for the summer. She stopped off in Reno and spent the night! We're flying out in the morning together."

Ivy forgot the tent mate's name the moment it was said. Was it Emily? Or Milly? Or Molly?

She was concentrating on the amber-colored eyes and the slight smile that tent-mate-to-be had offered and then suddenly withdrawn as she recoiled in horror at Ivy. "What happened to your . . . your shirt?" she said. "Did you have an accident or something?"

Ivy looked down. Smears of turtle blood and gravel had wrecked the front of her blouse. Not that it was a very good blouse to begin with.

"It's . . . I'm fine," Ivy struggled to explain. "It's just—I found an injured desert tortoise by the side of the road and I was trying to save him, and I guess . . . I guess he bled all over me!"

Annie and the tent mate had put on the short-sleeved polo shirts that the camp required its girls to wear. The shirts were blinding white with the green Allegro crest on the breast pocket, and the shorts were green with a white *A* monogrammed on the hem.

Annie took Ivy by the hand and led her to

the porch, although Ivy knew the way perfectly. In the hall Ivy nearly tripped over the two identical green duffel bags. They were labeled CAMP ALLEGRO, CRAWFORD NOTCH, NEW HAMPSHIRE, and strapped up with canvas web belts, ready for their trip east.

Ivy fixed her eyes again on the words under the Allegro crest on the two identical white shirts, still with their folds from the camp store's supply packs: FORTIETH ANNIVERSARY CAMP ALLEGRO 1909–1949. The tent mate's eyes raced down Ivy's clothing twice. The eyes were now a little amused. Ivy felt like a snail.

Annie's mother served lemonade to the three girls out on the porch. Down in the valley, Ivy's family's whole house — a trailer — could have fit into Annie's screened-in porch twice over. Annie's house looked out over the Washoe mountains, and on a clear day you might see Lake Tahoe from the attic.

"I know you are already fabulous pals!" Annie's mother chirped. Did she know the chance of them all being pals was as likely as a snowball surviving on a griddle? Ivy wondered.

The tent mate nattered on about last summer's scandal. An Allegro tennis counselor had been caught in the woods with a canoe instructor from the boys' camp across the lake. What the two might have been doing among the New Hampshire pines had been on everyone's lips.

"The two of them were probably just holding hands and singing songs in the woods!" said Annie's mother, amused. But her smile said she knew better and that only got the tent mate started up again about how the boy counselor had been fired and the girl counselor shamed to tears by the Allegro camp director.

Ivy listened impatiently. She couldn't wait to tell them about the rattlesnake that had wound itself around the axle of her dad's pickup truck the night before. That was much more exciting than last year's camp gossip.

The tent mate brought out a bottle of nail polish. There was no room edgewise for Ivy to say a word. She couldn't talk around or over this Allegro girl, with her bright hair and camp talk. Annie seemed already transported to New Hampshire. The tent mate kicked off her shoes.

"They don't let you do your nails at Camp Allegro," she explained in Ivy's direction. "Allegro was founded by missionaries, and missionaries don't believe in nail polish."

Ivy curled her hands so that the tent mate would not see the rough condition of her fingernails, but the tent mate wasn't the least bit interested in Ivy's fingernails. Annie spread both hands on the flagstone floor, and the tent mate coated each nail with glowing polish. "You can't have nail polish or radios or movie magazines or hair curlers at camp," said Annie for Ivy's benefit.

"Even if your mom sends candy bars, you are honor bound to turn 'em in."

"But guess what!" confided the tent mate. "They can't take the polish off your nails if you put it on before you get there!"

"Remember the night last year," said Annie, "when we sneaked into Tent Seven and painted Frances McCall's toenails blue while she was asleep, and she didn't even wake up?"

Ivy sipped her lemonade and watched the nail polish appear on Annie's fingertips in two lovingly applied coats.

Annie turned to Ivy and finally asked, "So, Ivy, besides injured turtles, what are you up to?"

Ivy took a deep breath. Her turn. The tent mate concentrated on the nail polish, fanning Annie's fingertips dry. "Dad ran over a rattle-snake with his pickup!" she said. "A ten footer! It got coiled around his front axle. He had to get out and shoot its head off with a twenty-two!

"He drove home, and guess what Billy Joe Butterworth did! He crawled under Dad's tr͟ uncoiled the headless rattlesnake, skin and set the skin to dry up on the barn roof. by morning vultures took away what was lei͟ of the snake. Billy Joe just stood outside star- ing up there at the empty barn roof and saying words he was not allowed to say. Only thing the vultures left was the rattle. Billy said he could sell it."

The tent mate turned white as a dinner plate. "Rattlesnakes!" she said. "We don't have those in San Francisco!"

"Lucky my dad saw it," said Ivy. "It could have come off the axle and bit his leg. Dad would have been dead in thirty minutes. He was an hour up Mule Canyon, pickin' up a dead buck for the mountain patrol. Nobody around."

The tent mate was horrified. "I don't want to hear any more about rattlesnakes or guns or

18

dead bucks!" she said. "Now I'm going to have nightmares about poisonous snakes getting into my bed!"

"There's no rattlers up here near the house," said Annie. "We're too high. Above the snake line. It's kind of like the tree line."

"There's no such thing as a snake line," Ivy said. "There's rattlers and sidewinders, even scorpions, all over the—" Annie shot Ivy a dark, warning look that said *Stop now!* She tried to steer the subject back to a bus trip up Mount Washington and how many choruses of "Ninety-nine Bottles of Beer on the Wall" had been sung on the bus.

But it was too late. The tent mate's hands shot up to her face. "Scorpions are poisonous!" she gasped. "They crawl out of the shower drains and bite you before you even know they're there! You can die!"

"The Nevada ones aren't so bad," said Ivy.

14

She looked at Annie's face. That remark had not redeemed her for the rattler story. She decided not to tell the tent mate that Billy Joe Butterworth liked to capture scorpions and make them fight in mason jars while he watched. Annie knew about Billy Joe's scorpion matches, of course. But Annie didn't want any more snake or scorpion talk. That was clear from her expression.

Ivy picked up the three lemonade glasses and carried them down the hall and into the kitchen. Annie's mother was carefully arranging fruit in a silver bowl. In went a pear, and then the pear was removed in favor of a peach. She looked up and saw Ivy's face.

"Honey," she said, "I'll miss seeing you around here this summer. You, too, I'll bet."

Ivy tried and failed to smile sunnily at Annie's mom. "I'll miss you a whole lot, too," she said. It was about all she could say. This kitchen was as much home to her as her own. Annie's mother as much mother to her as her own mom. It had been that way as long as she could remember.

"How's your mom?" asked Annie's mother, as she always did.

"Workin' hard," said Ivy.

"And your dad?"

"Him, too. Lots of guests coming this summer."

"How's that Butterworth boy? Making trouble?"

No answer from Ivy. She washed out the glasses vigorously at the kitchen sink and stood them on the drain board.

Annie's mother put down a nectarine and settled a hand on Ivy's shoulder. "Summer camp friends are like summer breezes," she whispered. "Come the end of August, Annie will say good-bye to all her camp friends and settle back into her regular life. Now, Ivy, you'll stay and have supper, won't you? We have lamb chops! Your favorite."

16

Ivy shook her head. "We've got three guests at the ranch this week," she answered. "Gotta help out. But thank you all the same."

Ivy strolled back down the hall with a plate of cookies. Annie's mother had covered the flagstones on the porch floor with a scarlet-and-brown rug. Two more of these rugs hung in frames on the wall. They were museum pieces, according to Annie's mother, two hundred years old and too delicate to be walked on. In the corner Annie and the tent mate had settled into a game of Old Maid, pairing up farmers and milkmaids. Somewhere in the deck was that fatal mateless card, the old lady with the crazy hair, forever alone in the world.

The tent mate's shoes still lay where they had been kicked, near the radiator. The deeply shined uppers were hand-stitched to the welt, the leather glove soft. Ivy could see inside the words *Ferragamo — Italy* in gold script. They were tempting as chocolates. Without think-ing, Ivy slipped off her sneakers and put the soft brown shoes on. They fit her as if they had been made for her. She marveled at their comfort. How much would it take to buy shoes of this kind? Probably a whole month of her dad's pay.

Annie's voice came a little sharply. "Ivy! What are you doing in those shoes?"

"Oh, sorry," said Ivy. She blushed horribly. "They were so beautiful. I only . . ."

Annie glared. *Please don't embarrass me even more after that half-dead turtle and rattlesnake busi-ness,* was what her eyes said.

The tent mate shrugged and went back to sorting her cards. "You want 'em? You can have 'em. They're my sister's, anyway."

Ivy so wanted the Italian shoes. She wanted to keep them on her feet forever. She wanted to hear the musical squeak of the heels. She wanted to own something that was not scrimped for, dollar by dollar, and bought at the end-of-season sale in the Sears Roebuck catalog. She kicked the shoes off quickly, as if they burned, gathered up her sneakers, and ran out of the room without saying good-bye. She dashed out to her bicycle, which was leaning against the house.

"Good-bye!" hung in the porch air for a moment. It was the tent mate's voice. Then Annie came out.

"Ivy, I'm sorry," Annie said. "But, jeez Louise, you make us look like hicks out here with your rattlesnakes and scorpions. Emily Hopkins is from San Francisco. Her family owns the Mark Hopkins Hotel. Of course she has Italian shoes! Do you have to act like you've never laid eyes on anything but Keds before? Do you have to mention all that snake stuff? Emily Hopkins is going to think we live in Outer Mongolia, and she's going to tell everybody at Camp Allegro that we're a bunch of hillbillies!"

Small tears pricked the corners of Ivy's eyes. "Have a good summer," she murmured before her voice failed her altogether.

Annie sighed. Her arms were folded. "Just in front of Emily, could you please not . . . ?" she began, but Ivy turned her bike so that Annie would not see her eyes and pedaled down the driveway. As she made the last turn, she remembered the turtle and pedaled quietly back. She heard two voices from the porch lifted in one of the Camp Allegro anthems, "Ever by Allegro's Shore."

Ivy knew all the words. Annie and she would sing them each summer when Annie came back from camp. In return, Annie always wanted to know everything she'd missed in town during her summer away. Would that comfortable trade ever happen again?

Ivy wandered back to the lawn and found the turtle much as she had left him, but with his feet and head now out. Again she placed him in her bicycle basket as gently as she could, then coasted downhill, letting the pedals spin on the way down. Tears blurred everything. *Why did I have to bring that up about the rattler? Why did I even touch those shoes? That stupid girl's going to think I'm worse than a dumb boy! Why, why, why didn't I keep my mouth shut about the rattlesnake and Billy Joe? Why did I let this stupid turtle wreck my shirt today?*

Ivy didn't care if Emily Tent Mate did find a rattler in her bed. She rather hoped she would find at least a garter snake. It was her best friend she cared about. She had disappointed Annie. Ivy had said and done three embarrassing things that could not be undone or unsaid. She and Annie had never had a fight before. Annie would fly away in the morning. It was too late to put things back together.

"Honey, what in heaven's name is that?" asked her mother when Ivy brought the turtle into the kitchen.

"I can fix him, Mom," said Ivy. She turned on the water in the kitchen sink and let it run into the bloody wound on the turtle's side, washing off the rest of the road grit. She placed him on the table under the brightest light. Then she took glue and pieced the hanging carapace sections together, covering them with duct tape.

Ivy carried the turtle to a shaded grass pen behind the barn, once home to a litter of farm pups. She filled a dish with water and broke an egg, leaving the yolk in half a shell not far from the water. The tortoise would either be dead or dig himself out by morning. Ivy knew that.

As she checked the patched-up shell one more time, a head with a shock of uncombed red hair appeared from around the barn. It was Billy Joe Butterworth.

"We gotta serve dinner," he said. "Your mom said to come get you."

"It's you that wants me, Billy Joe," said Ivy, " 'cause you're too lazy to do any chores alone. I know you. I'm taking care of this turtle, so go on and peel carrots and shell peas. 'S good for you."

"Well, you better come soon," he said. "There's more than one person's share of kitchen prep to do. And there's blood all over your shirt."

Ivy knew that Billy Joe would deliberately leave all the onions for her to weep over.

When Billy Joe left, Ivy grabbed a plain T-shirt from the clothesline. In the barn she ripped her worn-out Sears Roebuck blouse with the turtle blood into angry shreds and hid the pieces in an old feed sack where her mother would never find them. She cried there, in

24

the darkness of the barn. Angry loud sobs. Through the cobwebbed window she saw the turtle extend its legs, then its head, and move to the dish of water, where it drank deeply. Ivy dried her red and smarting eyes on her sleeve and headed for the kitchen. She'd start right away on the onions, and no one would ask her what the matter was.

While Ivy chopped Vidalias into fryable chunks, she skimmed yesterday's *Carson City Star,* which was folded under the onions to catch the juice. The paper ran a story about the rodeo, coming soon to town. Billy Joe would want to go to that. Billy Joe wanted to be a rodeo rider when he grew up, even though his mama would allow no such thing in the world. The newspaper ran the usual graduation speeches, reported from Carson City High. There had been a robbery at a pawn shop at the edge of town. She flipped through the sports and the obits pages. There was a full-page advertisement for a sale on birthstone friendship rings at Steinway's department store.

Ivy read the ad with interest.

Just three days before, on the final day of school, Mary Louise Merriweather had jounced into the fifth-grade classroom sporting one of those friendship rings with a honey-colored topaz in the setting. Blond and bouncy Mary Louise was the head of the popular girls. Ivy figured she'd been born to that destiny.

The idea was to buy a ring with your best friend's birthstone and give it to her. Then she'd buy one for you.

At the time Ivy had whispered, "Fakest things I've ever seen!" within earshot of Mary Louise, who was making one of her bubble-bath fusses over someone's ring. For a second Mary Louise had turned and bounced her curls in Ivy's direction, giving her a look that said, *I'll get you back for that remark!* But there hadn't been time for Mary Louise's revenge because school was out the very next day.

Tourmaline was Annie's birthstone. *Maybe, just maybe, Annie would forgive me if I sent her one of those rings while she's at camp!* thought Ivy. *But how will I ever get the five dollars?*

Money was scarce in Ivy's household. Her mother had ten marked envelopes that she kept for each of the household expenses. Into these envelopes went dollars that could never be spent for anything other than what was written on the envelope: groceries, electric bill, and so on.

Asking her mother about a raise in her allowance would likely only get her another twenty-five cents a week, if that. She asked anyway.

"My Ivy wants something," said Ivy's mother, forking the frying chicken around in a pan.

"I want to buy a ring," Ivy answered. "A sterling silver Tru-Friendship ring. They're on sale for five dollars at Steinway's. All the girls have them."

"Wait a few years, dear heart," said her mother. "The day may come when you marry a millionaire! Then you can buy a diamond ring set in platinum."

But Ivy didn't want to marry a millionaire. She didn't want to marry anyone. And she didn't want to wait.

Her father had no money to spare for a ring, either. Ivy pushed the coins from her last allowance across the kitchen table.

"Dad," she whispered hoarsely, "could you maybe put this in the slots at the gas station and see what happens? Maybe you'll get lucky and win a jackpot! Please?"

Her father smiled and pushed the money back. Nevada, of course, was the gambling state. There was a slot machine or two in every corner store. But Ivy's parents frowned on gambling, as did most of her classmates' families. The house odds were heavily stacked against every tourist with a cup full of nickels. Everyone in Nevada knew it.

"You don't want to ever start that, honey," Ivy's dad said, shaking his head. "Start with a dime, and an hour later you're broke." He finished his root beer and put the glass in the sink. "Whyn't you go on over to the Methodist church? Take a peek at the community board. See if anyone maybe needs a babysitter. You can make twenty-five cents an hour rockin' some cradle." He smiled sweetly at Ivy and held his rough rancher's hand against her cheek for a moment, as if the hand could say something that he could not.

Ivy couldn't explain to her parents how important this ring would be. Not only had Mary Louise Merriweather given the rings her popular-girl blessing, but Annie would surely forgive her if Ivy were to give her one. What's more, when school began again, Annie might return the favor and get Ivy a ring of her own. That would make the turtle blood, Italian shoes, and rattlesnakes go away.

Ivy's mother and father were not inclined to listen to fifth-grade anguish. "They'll forget all about those silly rings by September," Ivy's mother would say. But Ivy needed that ring for Annie more than anything in the world, and she had to find a way to get her hands on five dollars.

After supper was served and cleaned up, and her mother's feet were soaking in an Epsom-salt footbath, Ivy wandered outside to the near paddock. She was a terrible babysitter. More than once she'd gotten lost in a book while the baby howled at her to play with rubber blocks. She hated babysitting.

Instead, maybe she could stick the price labels on dry goods at Mr. Strunk's general store and sweep out the back room. The thought of indoor work in Mr. Strunk's dusty stockroom made Ivy's eyes close.

"If I had one wish on a magic lamp to start a business of my own, what would I want it to be?" she said aloud to Texas, one of the Red Star Ranch's best trail horses. Texas plodded over to Ivy and nudged her shoulder. As she went back inside to get him a carrot, the answer came to her.

When she was finished, Ivy showed her advertisement, carefully typed on Billy Joe's mother's typewriter, to her mom and dad.

"Good girl!" they said.

On Monday, Ivy tacked up one advertisement on the town hall bulletin board, posted one in the feed store, one in the A & P, and one on the post-office door.

```
IVY TAKES CARE!
I will care for your dog or pony,
snake, turtle, fish, cat, or bird
while you enjoy your vacation.
Experience and references provided.
Please call Carson 6-5153
```

Ivy waited a week. The phone in their house was on a party line of six families. All the calls seemed to be for somebody else. But Tuesday morning at breakfast, when she wasn't even listening for it to ring anymore, a call came for Ivy.

"This is Mrs. Pratt calling," said a cheerful voice on the other end. "We live on Indian

Springs Road, two miles from Mule Canyon. I saw your sign in the post office."

"How can I help you, Mrs. Pratt?" asked Ivy.

"Next week, Mr. Pratt and I are going to Mexico," Mrs. Pratt explained. "Our pony, Chestnut, will need care while we are away. Do you have experience with horses?"

"I learned to ride before I could walk, Mrs. Pratt," answered Ivy. "My dad's the stable manager at Red Star Ranch." Ivy liked the sound of *stable manager* better than *stable man of all work*.

Ivy knew just where Indian Springs Road met Mule Canyon. That afternoon she got out her bicycle. As she was about to go, Billy Joe Butterworth poked his head around the side of the house.

"Where are you going so fast, Little Miss Climbing Vine?" he asked.

"That's for me to know and you to find out!" Ivy snapped back.

Billy Joe had to know everything in the world. He couldn't stand it if he was out of the hearing zone of every detail of everyone's business. He even listened in on the party line to other people's phone calls. At least he did until his mother caught him one day, yanked the receiver out of his hand, and slammed down the telephone. Billy Joe was now careful only to lift the receiver when his mother was out of the house.

Ivy sped off. She knew Billy Joe could not follow her because he had left his expensive Schwinn bike out in the rain one too many times and the gears had rusted beyond his riding it ever again.

Mrs. Pratt opened her white picket gate for Ivy. Ivy parked her bicycle neatly, using the kickstand, although she usually just leaned it up on a fence. She gave Mrs. Pratt her letter of recommendation.

June 21, 1949

Red Star Guest Ranch
State Highway 61
Carson City, Nevada

To whom it may concern,

This is a letter of recommendation for Ivy
Coleman. Ivy's mother is our ranch cook. Ivy's
daddy is our man of all work. Ivy knows her
way around quarter horses, driving horses,
dogs, cats, and everything else on four legs.
She's a sensible girl! Honest and dependable.

Yours truly,

Cora Butterworth

Prop., Red Star Guest Ranch

Ivy gave Chestnut a sugar lump off the flat of her hand. Chestnut breathed right into Ivy's face and nudged her with his snowy, velvet nose.

Mrs. Pratt showed Ivy all the things she had to know about Chestnut. "And if you ever need help, why, you just call Dr. Rinaldi, the veterinarian down in Carson," said Mrs. Pratt. "You can't call us in Mexico. The phones down there are not something I would ask you to tackle."

Ivy smiled in relief. Calling Dr. Rinaldi in town was just fine by her. The vet often came up to the Red Star Ranch to give a horse a shot of bute or look at a split hoof.

Mrs. Pratt ran her hand down Chestnut's ample belly. "He's a little on the stout side. He needs some exercise," she said. "And don't forget to leave the radio on near his stall at night. He likes the radio. Especially *Music from the Stars* at six o'clock on KNEV."

Ivy wrote down every word Mrs. Pratt said and pinned her list neatly to the tack-room door.

"Do you think you can handle Chestnut?" asked Mrs. Pratt.

"A piece of cake, ma'am," said Ivy.

"How much do you charge?" asked Mrs. Pratt.

"I don't know," said Ivy.

"How about fifty cents a day?" asked Mrs. Pratt.

"That'll do fine!" said Ivy.

"Here is an advance payment," said Mrs. Pratt. "Don't spend it all in one place!"

Ivy did not mention the Tru-Friendship ring.

"I will see you next week, Chestnut!" said Ivy. The pony nickered at her. She gave him a palmful of sweet feed.

The following Monday, Ivy awoke early to the crow of the rooster. Mourning doves *coo-roo*ed in the cottonwood trees. In the distance, she heard the whistle of the train as it raced west across Nevada on its way to California. Mr. and Mrs. Pratt were on that train for the first leg of their trip to Mexico. For three weeks Ivy would be in charge.

The Pratts trust me completely, Ivy thought. *Without me, Chestnut would be alone in the world.*

She jumped out of bed and checked her shirt pocket for the sugar lumps she'd put there the night before. After she ate the breakfast that her mother had laid out the night before, Ivy went off to work on her bike. It was too early for slugabed Billy Joe Butterworth next door to have opened even one eye.

Chestnut was happy to see Ivy. Having smelled the sugar in her pocket, he made umpy noises. Ivy gave him one lump.

"Tomorrow you go on a diet, Chestnut," said Ivy. "I'm only going to bring you carrots from now on. We're going to slim you down a little!"

Chestnut lifted his hooves nicely while Ivy cleaned them. He stood patiently while she checked for bumps or scratches on his legs. He ate a flake of hay while Ivy brushed him. He made no trouble when Ivy put his blanket on his back, and he opened his mouth just so when she put in the bit of his bridle.

"Exercise time!" said Ivy.

Chestnut trotted gamely around his paddock, but when they got out of the gate, he stopped dead. No matter what Ivy did or said, the pony just stood his ground, flicking flies with his tail.

"I think it's because you are a fatty," said Ivy, "and you don't want to go uphill carrying me."

So instead of riding, Ivy walked beside Chestnut, leading him up the trail that wound over Mule Canyon. Chestnut made more umpy noises.

When they could see Washoe Lake sparkling in the rising sunlight from between the piñon pines, Ivy stopped. She let Chestnut drink from a stream that rippled down the mountain between the manzanita trees. They went home before the morning sun got too hot and the flies got too bad. Chestnut let Ivy ride downhill through the sage and yellow mallows.

Ivy put Chestnut's fly mask on and left him in his paddock.

In the late afternoon, Ivy returned and found Chestnut waiting for her in the shade of a stand of large cottonwood trees. In the shade there were no flies.

"Smart boy!" said Ivy. Ivy checked Chestnut for insect bites, and when she found one, she put purple gentian on it so it would heal. Then she washed the day's dust off him and brought him into his stall. She cleaned his water bucket and gave him another flake of hay while she checked his legs and feet.

Before lights-out, Chestnut got a handful of sweet feed and Ivy turned on the radio, tuned to station KNEV.

"Good night, Chestnut," said Ivy. "You are never really alone, because I will always come back."

Ivy made sure all the gates and stall door were closed before she bicycled home.

On the fifth day of work, Ivy got up the courage to spend Mrs. Pratt's five-dollar advance payment. After her Chestnut chores were finished for the day, Ivy went through town and stopped at Steinway's.

Ivy chose the ring with a tourmaline, which was Annie's birthstone. Her heart tripped as the precious money skidded out of her fingers and into Steinway's cash register. The Steinway's jewelry box felt hot in her pocket.

Ivy wore the ring home. For a moment after supper, she rested her hand on the windowsill where the stone caught the outside light and sparkled.

"Fancy ring," said Billy Joe, noticing, as he noticed everything. "Where'd you get the bucks for that little bangle?"

Ivy's hand disappeared into her pocket. "I don't see you wearing your fancy-dancy cowboy boots, Billy Joe!" she said. "Why not?"

Billy Joe gave Ivy a dark look and didn't answer. His uncle had given him a pair of hand-tooled western boots with silver tips for his tenth birthday. Because his feet were hot, Billy

Joe had kicked the boots off while sitting in the grandstand at a rodeo. The boots dropped to the soft dirt under the grandstand, where they stayed for about ten minutes before someone snatched them. Billy Joe had been made to string five hundred yards of barbed wire fence for losing the boots. It took him three days and some nasty cuts, into which his mom poured iodine. Ivy knew the whole story because the Butterworths' kitchen window was about ten feet from her bedroom window. She had the advantage of hearing all kinds of personal conversations, but Billy Joe had no such luck because Ivy's family's kitchen opened out onto the horse paddock.

The next day, Ivy put the ring into its box and the box into an envelope she swiped from the Red Star Ranch office. She addressed it to

Annie at Camp Allegro, Crawford Notch, New Hampshire.

The moment it went into the mailbox, Ivy was hit with the thought that if Camp Allegro forbade its campers from getting hair curlers and nail polish and candy bars in the mail, it would surely confiscate jewelry. Her heart sank, but it was too late. There was nothing she could do except wait for Annie's reply.

★   ★   ★

Each day brought new flowers to Mule Canyon and new weather to the sky. Ivy lost herself in the smells of horse and leather, and the memory of the turtle day faded. Along the stony Mule Canyon trail, bright claret-cup cacti opened their flowers. One day, Ivy found mule deer antlers behind a stretch of pines.

"A four-point rack!" said Ivy. "Dad'll like that for sure." She strapped the antlers to the back

44

of her saddle. Mr. Coleman collected them for ranch guests.

Each evening, Ivy mucked out Chestnut's stall. She cleaned his hooves, treated his fly bites, and gave him his sweet feed. Chestnut nuzzled her shoulder when she brushed him and talked to her in little horse grunts and sighs.

One night, just before she turned on Chestnut's radio, Ivy heard a squeak coming from an unused stall in the back of the stable. The mountains were full of critters of one kind or another, and Ivy knew that any number of them could creep into the barn if they liked and raid the sweet feed bin. Some creatures, like rattlers, were dangerous. Some, like skunks, were a nuisance, especially if your dog messed with them. Some, like coyotes, who stole lambs and anything else they could get their teeth into, were threats.

Most other critters, like jackrabbits, raccoons, and prairie dogs, were just out there, harmless and making a living like everyone else.

Quietly, Ivy edged down the sluiceway to the unused stall. She peered over its wall. On a heap of hay in the corner lay a red fox—a vixen—and six kits. A hole in one of the boards at the base of the stall must have been her way in, and there she had had her babies.

The fox's coat was the color of fire. She studied Ivy and showed her sharp teeth. Ivy studied her back and sensed the fear in her.

"What's wrong with that front foot, Mama Fox?" she asked.

On the floor, Ivy could see drops of blackened blood. She looked back at the fox's foot and spotted a blood-caked mass between the swollen pads.

Ivy looked deep into the fox's bright brown

eyes. She longed to lay a hand, for one second, on the snow-white hair in the creature's ears. This little red mother was needy, but she was also determined to take care of her kits.

Caring for wild critters was not something Ivy had been raised to do. Coyotes and foxes preyed on chickens and lambs. There was an Agriculture Department bounty paid to anyone who brought in a pair of ears and a tail. Still, Ivy believed the little fox family had a right to live, too.

"You beauty!" she whispered to the mother fox. "You beauty with your little kits, you'll have trouble finding food with that bad leg. I'll bring you something to eat and drink and get you through this." Ivy hoped her voice carried the same kind of comfort to the fox that it had for Chestnut. This time, the fox did not bare her teeth.

Ivy left the stable and went to a pine tree behind the Pratts' house. Out of a knot in the curled and prickly bark she took the spare house key off a rusty nail, where it was hidden.

The key worked perfectly in the kitchen door. Ivy found the icebox with no trouble. She held her breath and, joy of joys, there was a box of eggs with half a dozen still left. They'd go bad by the time the Pratts came home. She grabbed the box.

Ivy locked up and double-checked the door before she headed out to the stable. Without showing her face to the fox or making any noise she could help, she squatted down and rolled each egg into the stall so it ended up near the fox's tail. She followed this up with a dish of water, then left the stable. As she straddled her bike, Ivy paused to listen. She thought she could hear the crunch of an eggshell. All the while, the loopy, jazzy *Music from the Stars* serenaded both Chestnut and the stranger from the mountains with her tiny, hungry family.

The Red Star Ranch was not a fancy dude ranch like some of the big spreads in Nevada. It was just a workaday ranch that took on four guests at one time. All of the guests spent exactly six weeks on the ranch in their own little wooden cottage. Each had a bedroom with a single cot, an easy chair, a bathroom with a tin shower stall, and a front porch with a light that collected moths of all varieties. There were screens on the windows, and the towels were changed by Cora Butterworth once a week.

After six weeks, the guests went home, each of them with a Carson City judge's signed affidavit saying they had lived in Nevada for the required time. By the time they were home, they were no longer married to the person they'd been married to before they came. In 1949, Nevada, alone in the other forty-seven states, was the Divorce State.

But Ivy didn't know any classmates whose parents were divorced or who gambled good money down the drain in the slot machines. She noticed that the divorcing guests all seemed to come from places like New York City or Dallas or Miami. Ivy didn't think they were bad people. A lot of them were funny and nice. She guessed they had just made mistakes, and so they came to Nevada to unmake them. And while they were at the ranch, there wasn't a whole lot for them to do except go to the casinos, enjoy the mountain scenery from a saddle, and eat Ivy's mother's good cooking.

The guests seemed not to be members of the Clean Plate Club like Ivy and Billy Joe's families.

At dinnertime, they left drumsticks uneaten, steak half-finished, beans in a pile at the edge of the plate. Almost all of these leavings went to the two ranch dogs, Hoover and Coover, who waited out on the porch, thumping their tails, anticipating their treats.

"You have to share now!" Ivy told Hoover and Coover the night she'd discovered the fox. She took some bones and chicken wings and baked potatoes from the dogs' dishes, wrapping the best bits of meat in waxed paper. All for a wild creature and six furry red babies in a horse stall, a couple of miles over the mountain.

Then she looked up inflammation in *The Home Vet* and saw that the remedy for most pets was a baby aspirin. There were plenty of aspirin in the medicine closet. She started slipping one quarter of an aspirin a day into a steak rind or a chicken morsel for the fox, so the swelling in her foot would heal.

★　★　★

One afternoon, Billy Joe saw Ivy putting some waxed-paper-wrapped meat in her bike basket. She had wrapped the T-bone in the paper, sealing it with Scotch tape, neat as a butcher's package.

"Where are you taking that meat?" he asked from behind one of the wooden pillars on the porch.

"Trouble trouble, and trouble will trouble you, Billy Joe," said Ivy.

Billy Joe paused a beat. Ivy knew that he knew that she would never answer him. So he got more personal.

"Where's that fancy ring of yours, Miss Climbing Vine?"

"I took it back to the store because I decided I didn't like it," she said in what she hoped was a bored grown-up voice.

Billy Joe sashayed backward into his house with a knowing laugh. "I bet it was for your buddy back East at that camp of hers! I haven't seen any postcards from Camp Pellagra yet this summer, and I pick up all the mail every day!" he teased.

That hurt because it was true. Ivy had not heard from Annie yet. "Shut up, Billy Joe," said Ivy. "And it's *Allegro*, not Pellagra!" Was there no limit to his busybodyness?

Ivy biked to the Pratts' place with the small sting still inside her. It started to thunderstorm, so first Ivy brought Chestnut in from the rain. Then she tossed the leftover T-bone to the fox mother, whose foot looked worse today. She limped over to the piece of meat, and her eyes did not look bright. The kits cried around her.

"I'm worried about you, Mama Fox," said Ivy. "We can't have you leaving those kits hungry!"

Suddenly Ivy heard truck tires crunch into the stable yard, then the slam of a door. Dashing into the barn, rain pouring from the rim of his ten-gallon hat as if it were a gutter spout, was Dr. Rinaldi. Dr. Rinaldi had known Ivy from his visits to the Red Star Ranch since she was knee-high. The vet shook off the rainwater, smiled, and put a hand on Ivy's shoulder.

"I promised Martha Pratt I'd look in on you now and then," he said. "Make sure everything was running smoothly."

"Chestnut's fine," said Ivy. She did and didn't want to tell him about the foxes. Most people did not believe in nursing wild creatures.

The vet pulled Chestnut's ear affectionately and gave him a once-over. "Everything looks shipshape," he said, eyes on the clean stall and the neat stable.

"Since you're here, Dr. Rinaldi," said Ivy, "could you look at Chestnut's front right leg? He's had a festering horsefly bite there all week."

Dr. Rinaldi scrambled around in his bag and pulled out some ointment. He applied it, grumbling about horseflies being like a plague of locusts. Chestnut stamped and snorted at him.

"You bike over here?" the vet asked.

Ivy nodded. Then she looked up at the doctor. It was now or never. "Dr. Rinaldi, can I ask you something?"

As if on cue, a soft cry came from the spare stall at the back of the barn. Dr. Rinaldi cocked his head and looked at Ivy. Then he sauntered over to the spare stall and took a long look inside.

"Oh, my stars," he said.

"It's wild critters," said Ivy. "I know I shouldn't feed 'em, but she's doing poorly and the kits are hungry."

Dr. Rinaldi's eyes flickered from Ivy to the foxes and back again, taking it all in. "Mama's got an infected front pad," he said. "She won't make it without help."

"I know," said Ivy. "I've been giving her aspirins in scrap food."

Dr. Rinaldi strolled thoughtfully to the tack room and took down a three-inch-wide saddle girth from a peg. Then he opened his medical bag. "First we'll need a tranquilizer," he said. He prepared a needle and gave it to Ivy. "Want to give the injection?" he asked. Ivy had never held a shot needle in her life.

"Now, you gotta move quick while I hold her down," he said. He opened the stall to the harsh, scratching growl of the mother fox. Lightning fast, he drove the kits into a corner and threw himself over the fox's body, pinning her down across the head and shoulders with the hard leather girth. The kits mewed and scattered.

"Shoot her in the rump!" he instructed Ivy. "Right there on the larger muscle. Quick, now!"

Ivy felt a rush of blood to her head. With his legs, Dr. Rinaldi protected Ivy against the fox's flailing rear paws with their razor-sharp nails. Aiming at the silky haunch, she plunged the needle, releasing its contents into the fox's body. Within seconds, the animal relaxed and went quiet.

Dr. Rinaldi examined the fox's front paw. With a tweezer, he pincered out a spike of rusty barbed wire. Then he cleaned the foot and took out another hypodermic. "Antibiotic. You want to do another?" he asked Ivy.

She nodded.

This time Dr. Rinaldi showed Ivy how to prick the needle into the rubber top of the medicine vial and draw the medicine into the glass. Then he showed her how to check the full needle for air bubbles and get rid of them by popping it with her finger.

"Here is the muscle," he said, placing Ivy's fingers on the correct place on the fox's withers to inject. "Here. Right here. Just shoot it in."

She did exactly as he instructed. The red liquid flowed easily into the sleeping fox.

Ivy laughed. "I didn't think I could do it," she said. "But it was easy. I thought I was afraid of needles, but I'm not!"

"You know something, Ivy?" said Dr. Rinaldi. "You're good at this."

"Good at it?" asked Ivy.

"You've got instinctive hands and a way with animals," said Dr. Rinaldi. "Those are things a person is born with. You can't learn them. Ever since you brought that half-dead rabbit for me to fix when you were four years old, I said to myself, that girl's got good hands, nerves of steel, heart of gold. That's what makes a vet. Ever think about it?"

"Being a vet, like you?"

"Why not?" Dr. Rinaldi asked. There was no joke in his eyes. "I have no doubt in my mind that you could. Most people are driven by what other people expect. You've got a purpose of your own."

For one moment, Ivy felt everything small in her life fall away, as if she were already a vet, just like Dr. Rinaldi. Then she took a deep breath of reality.

"If I could ever afford to go to college," she said. "But that's a lot of money. My folks just get by."

Dr. Rinaldi smiled. He began packing his medical bag, capping the glass syringes carefully so they could be sterilized and reused.

"You'll make it. With a little spit 'n chicken wire, same as me," he said.

"And you have to be smart," added Ivy.

The doctor laughed. "You were born bright as a tree full of owls, girl," he said, running his hand over the silky red coat of the mother fox. She was already beginning to stir. Ivy placed the kits on the vixen's belly, where they squirmed and drank gratefully.

Dr. Rinaldi watched her. "Some people are just meant to do certain things," he said with seriousness. "You were fixed in heaven to do vet work, Ivy. Someday you will. Sure as Sunday."

By then, the storm had cleared. Dr. Rinaldi walked out into the sunny yard, his boots making a satisfactory clopping on the cobblestones. He tossed his vet bag into the back of his pickup. The truck bed was full of cow slings, large forceps, and other mysterious equipment.

"Go on home, now. Your ma'll have supper waiting. Cut out the aspirin. These pills are better, and throw in one of these antibiotic tablets with her hamburger every day. That critter'll come around quick," he said. Then he got into his truck and started the engine. It sputtered and choked to life. Out the window he said, grinning, "Now, you're not going to tell a living soul I used an expensive antibiotic on a wild critter, are you? Your dad'd laugh me out of his barn."

"Cross my heart and hope to die," answered Ivy.

Biking home, Ivy felt the sun warm her face. She cruised up Mule Canyon hill, pedals flying with no effort at all.

The world was full of invisible powers. There was, across the state of Nevada, the power of the slot machines. Those were called one-arm bandits, and they had the power to make people drop their money into a black hole of nothingness.

There was Annie's San Francisco tent mate. She had the power to make Annie into someone entirely other than who she'd been just the day before.

And then there was the power Ivy had discovered in Chestnut's stable. It was the power to bring back life and to stop suffering. That power was Dr. Rinaldi's. Maybe it could be hers, too.

When the supper dishes had been cleared and Ivy sat down to her summer reading, her mother scooted her chair over.

"Honey, your dad and I were talking," Mrs. Coleman said softly.

Ivy waited for the direction of this wind.

"When school starts again, we want for you to keep up some to the other girls, with their nice things."

"It's all right, Mama," said Ivy.

"We're real proud of you having a job," her mother added, looking down at her feet, taped up with special Dr. Scholl's supports. "So, Dad and I did a little calculating last night."

Ivy's mother reached over to the desk and picked up an envelope from her bill-paying file.

"This is a new envelope," her mother said. She turned it over so that Ivy could see it. The word *Ivy* was written on it in her mother's careful, Palmer-method penmanship. "Cora's full up with guests till November. Let's hope they're rich guests who tip Dad nicely and maybe leave something in the kitchen for me."

Everything depended on tips. The guests left room tips on their pillows when they left. These were collected by Cora Butterworth. But Ivy's dad took the guests riding into the mountains. If some New York City fellow found a nice rack of antlers for over his fireplace without having to kill a buck, her dad was likely to get a consideration at the end of the guest's six-week stay.

During the winter months, when the guests were few, Ivy's dad rode out on the trails, planting racks of sun-bleached antlers. If the squirrels didn't gnaw them to pieces, he'd know exactly where to find them in the summer.

"Well, look at what we've got here!" he would always say, pulling up his horse. Then an excited guest would jump off Texas's or Mirabel's back, pull the rack of antlers out of the brush where it had been carefully posed, and struggle it onto the saddle ring, where Ivy's dad solemnly tied it.

This was usually worth a couple of dollars, handed over at the end of the ride. Once in a while, if Ivy's mother cooked a guest's favorite dish just right, that guest might leave a silver dollar under their dinner plate.

With two fingers, Ivy's mother removed and handed over a five-dollar bill.

"That's for the ring you want, honey. Don't want you snooted down by anybody."

But Ivy did not take the money. She had already bought the ring for Annie and mailed it, using up the five dollars Mrs. Pratt had given her—just about half of Ivy's entire salary for the job.

"Mama?" she asked. "How much does it cost to go to the U.?"

"The university?" Mrs. Coleman looked over her glasses at Ivy, the five dollars still in her fingers.

"I want to save for college," Ivy said. "I want to go."

Her mother gulped. "Why, I'd guess the U.'s more'n four hundred dollars a year for tuition and board, honey. They've upped it from three hundred fifty. It was in the paper last week."

Ivy's father had been listening while cleaning the mud from his boots over a piece of newspaper. "Doctor or lawyer?" he asked, as casually as if he were commenting on the weather.

"Vet," said Ivy.

"Well, let's put the five dollars back," said Ivy's dad, "and write a big *U* on that envelope."

Ivy cracked open her book and threw her legs over the arm of her favorite chair. Ivy's mother returned the bill to the envelope, put the envelope back in the desk drawer, and turned the key. In this way the future was settled.

The fox kits seemed to grow up by the day. They were playful, and their red coats shone with good health. As far as Ivy could tell, the mother fox's foot had healed quickly. After a few evenings of treats dropped over the side of the stall, the vixen had lost her fear of Ivy, and she now padded over to catch whatever Ivy tossed in. The kits yipped happily at her arrival.

If Ivy had not been respectful of the fox mother and her wildness, she would have tried to sit with the kits and play with them for hours, but she never touched them. "It's better if you fear people," she told them. "People will try and kill you, so you must go back to your life in the desert."

Two nights from the time the Pratts were to come home, Ivy pedaled on down to Chestnut's stable. She took the pony out and performed all her night chores. Then she took half a meatball sandwich and went over to the fox's stall, where she dropped it in, to the hungry pleasure of mother and kits alike. It was at that moment that she heard the stamping of another horse outside the stable.

Ivy froze.

She didn't have to wonder long who it was. She smelled his bubble-gum breath over the manure pile and other stable smells.

Through the cobwebbed tack-room window, Ivy saw Billy Joe tie Texas neatly to a ring on the outdoor wall and stride into the Pratts' stable.

"What are you doing here, Billy Joe?" asked Ivy, trying to sound casual.

"Whatcha got here?" he asked, hoisting himself onto a saddle rack and peering over the side of the stall. "Look at that! That's five bucks, maybe more, waiting for me like fish in a barrel. There's a five-buck-a-pelt bounty for foxes, and I could get two bucks each for those kits."

"Leave them alone," said Ivy. The mother fox opened her mouth like a cornered cat and chattered at Billy Joe. Tiny flecks of her angry spit glistened in the air.

Billy Joe climbed down from the saddle rack

and walked over to where the Pratts' shotgun hung on the wall.

"That's not your property. Don't even think about it," said Ivy. But Billy Joe was not to be turned away.

Ivy's heart pounded. He was going to shoot this little wild family that she had healed, fed, and so much loved. He was going to kill them, skin them, and take the pelts to the sheriff. He'd cash them in for bubble gum baseball card packs and the Roman candles he liked to set off in the mountains.

"Leave the gun alone and go home." Ivy said, her voice rising with panic. "This is *private property!*"

But private property was not an idea that Billy Joe understood. He tried to reassure Ivy, "Oh, I'll split the money with you, Miss Climbing Vine. Don't worry. I'm not a piker! Fifty-fifty! We can make close to twenty bucks between us, and you can get one of those fancy sweaters that Mary Louise wears to school."

"Billy Joe," she said, "if you don't get on out of here right now, I will *ruin* you!"

"Ruin me!" Billy Joe laughed. He snapped his bubble gum but did not yet reach for the gun. "And how would you go about that, Miss Climbing Vine?"

So that he would have to listen to her very carefully, Ivy whispered, "Billy Joe, do you know what *Joker!* magazine is?"

Billy Joe turned a shade of red. Everyone knew that *Joker!* was a magazine full of off-color humor. Completely and totally forbidden in the Butterworth house. "What of it?"

"You remember Mr. Cuthbert?"

Billy Joe squinted. It was hard to remember the guests' names once they left the ranch, unless there was something special about them. "So, what about him?" asked Billy Joe.

"When Mr. Cuthbert went home, he left a whole pile of *Joker!* magazines under his bed. I found 'em and hid 'em where no one knows but me. Billy Joe, if you hurt these critters, your mother is going to find those magazines under your bed someday soon, when you least expect it. And then she'll skin you alive for reading smut."

"You are lying, girl!" said Billy Joe.

"Try me," said Ivy.

Mr. Cuthbert had actually left a stash of *Time* magazines, not *Joker!* magazines, but Billy Joe couldn't guess that. Ivy knew a thing or two about Cora Butterworth, a deacon of the Methodist church. To Cora Butterworth, *Joker!* magazine would stand about as close to the Devil's work as ever came between two covers. Billy Joe knew it, too.

She could almost hear Billy Joe skim through the possibilities of what would happen to him if his mother found a pile of *Joker!* magazines under his bed.

Finally Billy Joe said darkly, "That's blackmail, Ivy. Blackmail."

"And that's murder," said Ivy, pointing to the gun.

Billy Joe did not linger. He walked out of the barn, untied Texas, threw the reins back over the horse's neck, and got in the saddle. Ivy watched his every move.

"Blackmailer!" he yelled, so Ivy was sure to hear it.

She watched him until his horse made a turn at the top of Mule Canyon, so she knew for sure he intended to go home. But she also knew that life in the stable was no longer safe for her foxes. The vixen mother padded gracefully around the stall, putting her full weight on the injured foot. Her family was ready for the outside world.

Ivy opened the door of the stall wide, got the hose, and aimed a jet of water above the foxes. "Go on, now!" she yelled.

The fox mother and her kits bolted out of the stall and into the stable. Another blast of the hose sent them out into the paddock. But then they stopped. They circled and watched her, as if they might get one more piece of steak.

Ivy picked up the gun and broke open the barrel. There was a cartridge in each chamber.

"Git! Git!" she shouted at them. "Go, little family! Don't ever come back!"

As she discharged the gun into the air, the fox mother and her kits lit out like red streaks for the mountain beyond. The last things she saw were two white tail tips disappearing behind the sagebrush.

Ivy piled up some stray cinder blocks to seal the hole where the mother fox had crawled into the stable. She ejected the used cartridge from the shotgun, then locked it and all the remaining cartridges in a drawer in the tack room. She didn't trust Billy Joe one lick.

"Stay out there, where you belong!" she yelled after the fox family and into the distance. She knew she would never see them again.

Monday morning, Ivy woke as her alarm clock hit five a.m. She heard the train coming eastward from California. The Pratts were on that train, coming home after three weeks away.

The night before, Ivy had made sure that Chestnut would be show-ring clean, with his mane braided, his hooves oiled, and his stall clean as a whistle when the Pratts' Pontiac turned into the drive.

Sure enough, Mrs. Pratt was thrilled to see her pony so fit and happy.

"I'll miss Chestnut," said Ivy.

75

"You may come anytime and say hello and enjoy him," said Mrs. Pratt, taking five silver dollars and a fifty-cent piece out of her purse and giving them to Ivy.

Ivy thanked Mrs. Pratt. "I would have taken care of Chestnut for nothing!" she added.

"That's the best kind of work, isn't it?" said Mrs. Pratt. "The kind you'd do anyway, for nothing. Don't spend it all in one place," she added.

"It all goes in my college envelope," said Ivy.

"I thought you'd say something like that," said Mrs. Pratt. "Honey, if you are going to run a business, you should get yourself a wristwatch. Strunk's carries a large variety of them. Here's another five dollars. Consider it a tip. Promise you'll get a nice watch for yourself, now?"

Ivy promised with a big smile. "You can call me anytime," she said. "I'll be here. And, thank you, Mrs. Pratt. I never thought I'd have a wristwatch till I graduated from high school!"

Ivy rode into downtown Carson City. She parked her bike at Strunk's General Store and clanked down her ten new silver dollars for Mr. Strunk's Savers' Club. If you put a dollar in the Savers' Club every month, Mr. Strunk gave back your twelve dollars at Christmastime and added a dollar interest, hoping you'd spend it in his store. But come Christmastime Ivy was going to withdraw her money with interest and put it all in the U. envelope.

"Well, if it isn't Miss Moneybags!" came a voice from the end of the soda fountain. This was followed by a loud snap of gum. Who else but Billy Joe Butterworth was looking right down the soda bar at Ivy with that superior expression on his face. "Making money hand over fist! How much did you get paid?" he asked with a snort. Ivy paid Billy Joe no mind whatsoever.

On one side of Strunk's front window was an array of Star Crazy watches. The tiny Star Crazy girl on the face of the watch smiled a movie-star smile, little jewels for eyes.

Ivy asked to try the watch on. Mr. Strunk was happy to let her try it in three different color band and jewel combinations. "I asked you a question, Miss Snoot!" said Billy Joe. "How much did those people pay you for walking that fat little horse around the paddock twice a day?"

Ivy plonked her arm down right in front of Billy Joe, who didn't own a watch, and never would, because his mother knew he'd lose it, break it, or dunk it in the rain barrel the very first day.

"That's for me to know and you to find out!" said Ivy.

Tick, tick, tick, went the watch. Billy Joe looked at it enviously. Ivy took the watch off and gave it back to Mr. Strunk. "I'll think about it," she said.

"I'll make you a deal," Billy Joe said.

"Yeah, what's that?" asked Ivy.

"I'll buy you a soda if you cross your heart and hope to die never to go in my room and leave anything there or under my bed!"

"Looks like you've learned a thing or two about private property, Billy Joe," said Ivy. "It's a deal. Providing you call me by my right name, *Ivy,* and never call me Miss Snoot or Miss Climbing Vine from here on in."

"Deal," said Billy Joe. He slapped the soda counter with the palm of his hand. "Two choco-late malts, please, Mr. Strunk! One for me and one for Ivy here."

"Make mine a double!" said Ivy.

Inca

Opportunity always knocks when you least expect it," Ivy's mother said, after Ivy complained that the telephone was not immediately ringing with new jobs. Ivy never would have guessed that her next assignment would come from one of the guests at the Red Star Ranch.

"Poor Mr. Burgess," said Ivy's father one July evening when the Red Star guests had been taken to the Christmas Tree Lodge for a fancy dinner. "I took him out on the Eagle River trail today. I showed him beautiful Washoe Lake, and all he did was cry. Comes from New Jersey. Terrible wife."

It went without saying that all the guests at the Red Star Ranch had terrible wives or terrible husbands, because that was the side of the story you got when you ran a dude ranch in Nevada in 1949.

Ivy's dad was a man who hated gossip. On the other hand, it was near impossible not to reveal details of the guests and their troubles, because it was all in a day's work and there were always interesting guests at the Red Star Ranch.

Ivy didn't usually listen in on conversations, but she drank in every word of what her dad told her happened along the trails. The guests usually spilled the beans about what was happening back home the second or third week they went out riding with him. That was how Ivy'd found out all about a certain Mr. Smith, who, by mistake, married a lady who liked to throw dishes at him and had run off with a traveling salesman.

Billy Joe Butterworth made it his business to know all about the guests. When he could, Billy Joe had been known to listen in on guests' conversations over the telephone line. He had been especially interested in a Mrs. Jones, married by mistake to a bank robber who ate nothing but garlic.

Billy Joe could hardly contain himself when a really interesting guest came along. He said he kept a book of all their doings and undoings, but Ivy didn't believe him because Billy Joe was too disorganized to write anything down, even in his school notebook.

Ivy waited for her dad to release a little more information about Mr. Burgess. Ivy's dad went on. "That poor sap, Burgess. Still boo-hooing like the world has come to its end."

"That big, handsome, barrel-chested man?" asked Ivy's mother. "Why, he ate three plates of pancakes for breakfast! I didn't have any more batter after him, not to mention all the bacon."

"And he's been here three weeks already," Ivy's dad added. "Most of 'em have calmed down some by this time."

"What kind of wife would leave such a handsome, sweet man? I'd like to know!" Ivy's mother said.

Ivy twirled a forkful of her spaghetti and wondered how much her daddy would tell about why such a man might have cried on the horse trails up in the mountains, where the desert flowers bloomed and Lake Tahoe shone like a diamond miles off on the California line.

"He misses his dogs is what," said Ivy's dad. "He don't like horses so much. He likes dogs. Dog breeder. He's got a whole kennel back home, and you'd think the dogs was his kids."

Late that night, Ivy was awoken by a low moaning sound coming from one of the guest cottages. For a minute she thought it might be a coyote who'd lost her kits. But if it was a coyote, Hoover and Coover would be on it in a flash, and they were quiet. The moaning grew louder.

Ivy sat up and listened. *I bet that's poor Mr. Burgess crying over his dogs. I bet I could cheer him up,* said Ivy to herself. She put on her jeans and T-shirt and slipped out the front door. On the way out she grabbed a handful of chocolate Hershey's Kisses from the candy dish, meant only for ranch guests. She let herself out and crossed the grassy patch that separated the guest cottages from the Butterworth's main house. Mr. Burgess occupied cottage number three. Ivy tapped politely on the door.

She had to tap louder before Mr. Burgess heard her. He opened the door, blowing his nose. "I'm so sorry if I disturbed you," said Mr. Burgess. "I'll be quiet."

"I brought you some Hershey's Kisses," said Ivy. "Sometimes when I get upset, my mama gives me one and I unwrap the silver paper and eat it and it stops the crying, *bam!*" She kept her voice low. The guest cottages were close to the Butterworths' house, and Billy Joe could hear a pin drop.

"Come in," said Mr. Burgess. "Why on earth should a nice girl like you cry?"

"Because Mary Louise Merriweather at school makes my life miserable because she's so perfect and snotty to everyone who isn't her friend," explained Ivy, "and my best friend hasn't written to me all summer from camp."

Ivy took a chocolate out of her pocket and offered it to Mr. Burgess. He peeled off the wrapper, popped it into his mouth, and sucked on it.

He wiped his eyes on the sleeve of his pajamas and sat on his bed.

"I'm a fool," he said. "A fool for my dogs. I came out here to divorce my wife and had to leave my German shepherds in Teaneck, New Jersey, with my brother."

"What are their names?" asked Ivy. She sat in the moonlight in the rocking chair opposite Mr. Burgess.

"Siegfried," he answered, blowing his nose with a neatly folded handkerchief. With each dog's name, his voice grew happier. "Birgit, Tristan, Elsa, and Parsifal. I trained them to be champions in the show and obedience ring. I have photos."

He turned on the light next to his bed and from his wallet on the dresser removed five photographs of five German shepherds. They all looked exactly the same to Ivy.

"Beautiful!" she said. "Especially that one!"

"That's Birgit," said Mr. Burgess. He unfolded a newspaper clipping, also kept in his wallet. It showed him with a winning team of shepherds at the Madison Square Garden Westminster dog show.

"Wow!" said Ivy. "That's the most famous dog show in the country!"

"I have only three weeks and three days before I see them again," Mr. Burgess explained, as if in Nevada he were the prisoner of Zenda. "My wife, Elma, thinks dogs are dirty and dangerous. She left me and fell in love with a banker who hates dogs and lives in a big modern apartment building in New York City and drives a yellow racing car."

"I'd be upset, too, Mr. Burgess," said Ivy. "I don't understand people who don't love animals. I actually run my own business. It's an animal take-care service. I do dogs, horses, turtles, birds — whatever people have."

"I wish Elma had taken lessons from you, Ivy," said Mr. Burgess. "Dogs are just creatures like us people, and I love 'em like my own kids. That is, if I had kids, which I don't, 'cause Elma doesn't like kids, either."

Ivy nodded in sturdy agreement. "I'd rather have five German shepherds than any old New York City banker," said Ivy.

"I would, too," said Mr. Burgess, his voice squeaking a little.

"I'll take the yellow racing car!" said a voice from the doorway. It was Billy Joe Butterworth, in his blue striped pajamas. He stood in the light of the porch lamp, batting at the moths that gathered there.

"Billy Joe, you get on out of here!" snapped Ivy. "This is a private conversation!" But it was too late. Billy Joe had already unlatched the cottage door and let himself into Mr. Burgess's room, cool as a cucumber.

"I have an idea!" Billy Joe said. "It's better than any old chocolate candy, too."

Ivy had half a mind to clock him over the head then and there, but he signaled her and went on. "Five miles south of town, there's a lady who's got five of them shepherd pups. Saw them today, 'cause my dad dropped off some hay at the Perkins place. Cute as day, those pups. Born end of May, I reckon. She's got a sign up now, advertising 'em. Maybe you'd like to see 'em just to cheer you up!"

Ivy knew what Billy Joe was up to. He was afraid Mr. Burgess might bolt right back to New Jersey to his dogs and not pay his bill if he was this homesick. Guests who didn't pay were bad news for the Red Star Ranch. Sometimes guests just skedaddled. Some guests got telephone calls and all their marriage troubles were forgiven over the phone. The whole ranch suffered when the divorcers kissed, made up, and went home. It was important to keep the guests happy. Unpaid rentals meant mashed potato sandwiches instead of ham-and-cheese for both Ivy's family and Billy Joe's.

Mr. Burgess looked at Billy Joe as if he had seen the second coming of the Lord.

"I'd love to see those pups," he said. "What time do you two finish day chores tomorrow?"

Ivy did not un-dignify the day by arguing with Billy Joe as to who would sit in the front seat of Mr. Burgess's rented Cadillac. A fancy car meant more to Billy Joe than it did to her. Ivy had it in the back of her mind that, just maybe, one of the Perkinses' pups might come home with Mr. Burgess and it might just as well ride in the backseat with her. Another dog wouldn't matter much at the Red Star Ranch. Hoover and Coover were eleven-year-old sheepdog brothers and didn't like to do much more than lie in the sun and chew the burrs off their feet. They didn't even get up for jackrabbits anymore.

"Boy, it must be fun to drive this baby!" said Billy Joe as Mr. Burgess put the car in reverse. Ivy knew this was Billy Joe's way of asking if Mr. Burgess would let him take the Caddy to the end of the driveway.

"It's a rented car, Billy Joe," said Ivy. "It'd cost a lot of money if something went wrong, like stripping the gears!"

Billy Joe turned around and gave Ivy a serious stink eye. He knew that she knew that he had stripped the gears on his dad's pickup and was forbidden to even put a hand on the steering wheel.

At the Perkinses' farm, Mr. Burgess vaulted into the middle of the puppy enclosure. Mrs. Perkins tossed an apron at him so his pants wouldn't get messed up.

"Champion bloodlines, dam and sire," she recited. "They got all their inoculations and are vet-certified in perfect health. Look at the bone on that one. Look at the bites. No over-shots, no undershots, no fiddle fronts, no straight stifles, and no laggy, draggy hindquarters in this madhouse!"

Ivy knew the words *dam* and *sire* meant the mother and father, the same as for horses. But she wondered about *straight stifles* and *fiddle fronts,* not to mention *laggy, draggy hindquarters.* Mrs. Perkins did not explain these things, but handed out sodas all around.

The price of the pups sounded like a small fortune to Ivy. Ivy guessed that Mr. Burgess, having rented a Cadillac when he might have rented a Chevy or a Ford, did not have too much trouble with money.

"How come the females are more costly?" asked Ivy.

Mrs. Perkins picked up a girl pup with a sherbet-pink tummy. "'Cause they're gonna give you a lot of litters," she answered. "Breed 'em and you'll get the price back ten times over in a jiffy. Not that we do it for the money, mind you!"

One after another, Mr. Burgess cuddled the German shepherd babies in his arms. As the afternoon grew late, it was clear he could not bear to leave without one. Finally after much backing and forthing, Mr. Burgess chose a male with a black saddle on his reddish-tan back, black stockings, and a black-as-charcoal muzzle.

On the way home, Ivy got to hold the pup in the backseat of the car. She held his front quarters on her lap and whispered in his out-sized ears. She stroked him under the chin. The pup curled up and went right to sleep with the rhythms of the stroking and the car swaying.

Mr. Burgess explained that *overshot* and *undershot* meant teeth not properly aligned. *Straight stifles* were hind legs with no bend at the knee, and *fiddle fronts* were front feet that turned out. "All these things keep a dog from working to the maximum," said Mr. Burgess, "and he won't be in a show ring for long if he's got any one of 'em."

"What about *slaggy, draggy hindquarters*?" asked Billy Joe.

"Lots of shepherds are slanted down in the back," said Mr. Burgess. "As if they were half sitting. It's a poor trait to breed into a dog. I don't like it."

Mr. Burgess peered into the rearview mirror

and smiled at Ivy, who held his pup in her lap. "All my dogs are named after German operas, but this one is different. He has a royal nose. I think he looks like the emperor Montezuma. I am going to call him Inca."

They stopped to buy a wire-sided dog crate at the feed store in Carson. Then home they went, with a car full of dog food and toys and a brand-new collar and woven leather leash for Inca. Ivy did not mention to Mr. Burgess that Montezuma was an Aztec, according to her history book.

"How come you put him in that box?" asked Billy Joe. "Seems like you're jailing him up, to me!"

"You'll see," said Mr. Burgess, stuffing a pillow and a towel into the crate. The next moment, Inca started chewing the pillow.

"No, Inca!" said Ivy, but Mr. Burgess said, "Put your hand in the crate with him, Ivy. Take the pillow out of his mouth. Say, 'Leave it!' and tap him on the nose sharply with one finger."

Ivy took the pillow from Inca's mouth and said, "Leave it!" over and over, tapping his nose and making her voice stern. "It's not working, Mr. Burgess," she said.

"It will," said Mr. Burgess.

After ten more times, Inca stopped bothering his pillow. He put his head between his paws and mooned his eyes Ivy-ward.

"Now praise him," said Mr. Burgess. "The treat is a message. It doesn't need to be bigger than a good-size pebble."

"Good dog!" Ivy said, giving Inca half a biscuit.

"He's learned two things," Mr. Burgess said. "Not to chew his pillow and the words *leave it*. Very important!"

"I want to do some stuff with him, too," said Billy Joe.

"Good!" said Mr. Burgess. "See that hill on the other side of the paddock? First give him some water, then take him for a run all the way up there. When you come back, look for ticks and burrs. Let him empty himself out, and then give him more water."

As Inca took off with Billy Joe, Hoover and Coover watched with cool eyes, barely thumping their tails in their sunny spots on the porch. Billy Joe sprinted up into the hills with Inca beside him. The puppy raced just as hard and fast as Billy Joe could go.

Cora Butterworth came out of the house. She stood and watched, hands on hips with a wet dish towel crammed in her apron. She grinned. "Mr. Burgess," she said, "you're good for that boy. He should run up there fourteen times a day, far as I'm concerned. Run the bejiggers out of him! Only time that boy isn't in trouble is when he's asleep or on the move."

Inca was happy to drink his water after his big run. Contented, Inca curled up in his cage with his pillow without once putting his teeth into it.

"That's enough for today," said Mr. Burgess. "We'll leave him here in my room and let him howl while we go to the big house and eat. He'll learn that yowling gets him exactly nowhere."

★　★　★

In the morning, Ivy played tug-of-rope with Inca, so he knew to play with the right toys and not chew up anything belonging to people.

Ivy could hear Mr. Burgess's screen door squeak open at six a.m., much earlier than any of the other ranch guests. He fed Inca outdoors and kept him out until he relieved himself so he didn't mess the house.

"The dog's master or mistress is in charge of what goes in and what comes out and when,"

Mr. Burgess explained to Ivy. Every time Inca was about to relieve himself, Mr. Burgess said the word *go* very loud. Then he praised Inca when he got it right. The first day was a Monday. By Wednesday, after hearing *go!* so many times, Inca got the picture. *Go!* was a clear command. He did not once mess up the house.

"All this eating and drinking and going to the bathroom outdoors!" said Ivy.

"That's the way," said Mr. Burgess. "It's a day's work training a dog, and you have to be as fair as a nun on a hockey field."

It was Billy Joe who took Inca for his big run every afternoon. It was Ivy who did the obedience training. She learned to loop a choke-chain collar the right way so it didn't hurt Inca's throat and taught Inca the command *heel* so he'd walk nicely at her side and not pull.

Ivy pushed down Inca's backside and taught him to sit, each time giving him a tiny bit of dried liver, which in Inca's mind seemed to be the snack food of the gods. When Inca got it right, she smoothed his soft red ears between her fingers and told him what a good boy he was.

"Oh, I wish you were mine!" Ivy whispered to him, but she knew there would be no expensive German shepherd show dogs in her future.

Ivy didn't give Inca too much to remember at once. *Heel* was easy. *Sit* took a few days, because Inca's tail was so waggy and he sat on top of it while it was going like a windmill, and then he'd fall over and bite his own tail to get it to stop.

Everyone in the guest lounge at the Red Star Ranch laughed at this, but Mr. Burgess held up his hand.

"No, please," he said, "dogs hate to be laughed at, so you'll just have to chuckle into your root beer so he can't hear you."

Mr. Burgess showed Ivy how to make Inca

lie down by putting the treat between his sitting front feet and giving it to him only when he lay down. *Down!* was hard. Inca was a big, squirmy puppy, and when Ivy pushed him down, he rolled over and kissed her.

"Don't let him do that!" said Mr. Burgess. "Training is work. Shepherds love work, and they understand when you take it seriously."

Come and *stay* followed on from *down.* "German shepherds live to serve," said Mr. Burgess. "They love to follow commands. So, when we're finished with the basics, we'll have Inca jumping hurdles and picking out the toy I want him to fetch from a whole pile of toys."

Mr. Burgess taught Ivy to teach Inca one new skill at a time, and they went over and over the commands until the puppy knew these were the most important words in his life. Ivy never used the word *no* because Mr. Burgess said everybody used *no* a thousand times a day, and the dog could not understand it after a while. *Leave it!* was a much clearer command.

"He's the best dog who ever lived!" Ivy said to Mr. Burgess.

"No," said Mr. Burgess. "He's just a good shepherd. They're all that way."

★　★　★

On the last night of Mr. Burgess's stay, everyone sat down to a So-Long-It's-Been-Good-to-Know-You supper, which was a Red Star Ranch tradition. Ivy's mother made leg of lamb and served it up to the guests with mint sauce. Inca sat by the sofa. He was not allowed to beg at the table and knew he would be banished from the room if he did. His gimlet eyes didn't miss a piece of the lamb as it went from guest fork to guest mouth. Ivy kept a little piece of gristle aside for Inca to have in the kitchen later, when he followed his *down* and *stay* commands.

Suddenly the telephone rang. It was for Mr. Burgess. When he returned to the supper table, his face was pale with worry. Sweat gleamed and beaded on his forehead. Ivy thought it might have been Mrs. Burgess making a nasty call. That would not have been the first time an unpleasant phone call had happened during supper at the Red Star. Maybe one of his shepherds at home was hurt or sick.

"Mr. Burgess?" said one of the new women guests, Mrs. Blanc. "If you don't mind my saying so, you look as if you'd seen a ghost!"

Mrs. Blanc was a peppy little lady whose husband had made her give up the piano, her one joy in life. Mr. Blanc had cut a hole in the side of their apartment house in Pittsburgh and pushed the piano out through the hole, crashing

107

it into the cement backyard, five stories down. This was according to Billy Joe, who happened, completely by accident, to run across one of Mrs. Blanc's letters after she'd thrown it in the trash.

Mr. Burgess leaned back in his chair and looked down the table at Ivy, who was serving vegetables to the guests.

"That was American Airlines," he said, his voice unsteady. "They have the vet's certificate that I sent them so that Inca can travel with me on the plane tomorrow. Trouble is, they won't take a pup this young. What am I going to do? I have to get home on tomorrow's flight. My brother can only stay with my shepherds at home in Teaneck till tomorrow night. Oh, holy moly mackerel, what am I going to do?"

Ivy knew the answer to the problem before she served the next spoonful of peas.

"Well," she said, "as you know, I have an

animal-care service, Mr. Burgess. I can take care of Inca until he's old enough to go. Then we'll put him on a plane and fly him to New Jersey, if you make the arrangements." She caught her mother's eye, and her mother nodded. More money in the envelope marked *U.* was a good step along the way.

"I'll help, too!" said Billy Joe.

All the color returned to Mr. Burgess's face. "You will?" he asked shakily. "It would be for almost three weeks."

"Sure," said Ivy. "I'll keep up his training, too."

"I'll run him up into the hills every day of the week," put in Billy Joe.

Mr. Burgess was so happy that he offered Ivy a ten-dollar bill and five to Billy Joe, right there on the spot.

"You don't have to do that, Mr. Burgess," said Ivy. "I never charge but twenty-five cents a day. Three weeks is just five dollars, twenty-five cents."

Billy Joe's eyes said, *Shut up, Ivy,* from across the room, but Ivy never shut up just because that silly boy wanted her to. She was saving her money for vet school. Billy Joe claimed he was saving his money for a beat-up motorcycle, except he never really saved it. He usually lost it in the laundry and his mother kept it, because she said all money found in the wash was hers to claim and give to the church, and if he didn't lose it, Billy Joe liked to spend every dime that came his way on bubble gum and fireworks.

Mr. Burgess made Ivy and Billy Joe keep the money. "Cheap at the price!" he said. "Besides, you'll need some of it for dog food. Now, I say root beer all around!" he announced happily.

When supper was finished, Mrs. Blanc went to the old, carved-up piano in the lounge. She banged out "Hark, the Herald Angels Sing," which was one of ten songs, all of them Christmas carols, that she said she knew how to play. Never mind it was only the middle of August.

Although she would never have cut a hole in the wall of a house herself, Ivy was not sure Mrs. Blanc's husband was completely in the wrong, back there in Pittsburgh.

Next to the training, the best thing about Inca was nights. Inca's crate was set up right next to Ivy's bed. Ivy stretched out an arm and went to sleep each night with one or the other of Inca's ears in her fingers. She talked the puppy down from the day's excitement, always ending with, "Oh, Inca, I wish you were mine." Ivy would never have a dog of her own. Her mother could tell her to the nickel just how much a dog would cost the family per year and would conclude by saying that they could not afford a dog like Inca in this lifetime.

Billy Joe Butterworth was a can't-sit-still boy if ever there was one, so he was not much for the repetitive work of dog training. Ivy recalled that he'd been the same way in third grade about his times tables. He couldn't and wouldn't and didn't remember them, until his dad made him recite them in the kitchen for one hour every night by the clock, so that he mightn't wind up as the village idiot. Somehow, those multiplication tables got etched into Billy Joe's brain like the Pepsi-Cola song on the radio, but it wasn't easy.

But Billy Joe faithfully helped every evening after chores with the big Inca run. Probably, Ivy figured, Billy Joe was afraid if he didn't work hard, she'd make him give Mr. Burgess's five-dollar bill to her, and he'd probably already lost that five-dollar bill. It was probably laundry-clean from being in Billy's Joe's dirty jeans pocket and was probably at that very minute in the church collection plate.

Mr. Burgess had shown Ivy how to make good use of a collection of old horse hurdles in the back of the barn. She set them up in a winter paddock. Using the command word *hup!*, she got Inca to go over a good four-footer with no trouble.

Ivy dreamed that one day Inca might be a Utility Dog Excellent, the highest rank in the dog training world, according to Mr. Burgess. She would have contributed to this. Maybe Mr. Burgess would find a big dog show out West and invite her to the ringside.

Ivy was just picturing this dream when Billy Joe's voice rang out, "Ivy! Mail for you!"

On top of the pile of bills and flyers was a

postcard. The picture side had a photo of Silver Lake in New Hampshire. In the lake was a squad of dark-green canoes, paddled by smiling girls, with *Allegro* in yellow script on the bows.

The message side simply read, *Hi! I'm having a great summer—wish you were here! Annie.*

That was it? Ivy turned the postcard over and over. What did it mean? It was like a message from a stranger. Did Annie really wish Ivy were there? There was no way to know. Summer was practically over! Still, it was better than no postcard at all. But the ring had not been mentioned. Had the camp taken it from its wrapping and held it aside? Had the United States Post Office failed to deliver it?

That night, Ivy's letter to Annie took up three pages, the maximum allowed for a three-cent stamp. She only hoped that Annie was not so caught up with canoes and campfires that she had lost interest in things from home. And she hoped the letter would make it to New Hampshire before Annie was turned around and already headed home.

In the morning, Ivy put the letter in their mailbox and turned up the flag. She was glad to be home, not in New Hampshire. She had seen the Allegro yearbook. Those eastern girls with their middy shirts and English saddles didn't compare to beautiful Inca. She called Inca to her side. Ivy had collected a mess of old toys from the Butterworths' attic and made Billy Joe put them in a bag, so the smell of her fingers would not be on any of them. It was all in a training book given to Ivy by Mr. Burgess, which Billy Joe had no patience to read.

Billy Joe was leaning both arms on the fence

behind her, chewing a piece of timothy grass. "What do you want those old toys for?" he wanted to know.

"You'll see," said Ivy. She rubbed a six-inch shank of rope with her hands for a minute. Then Ivy made Inca fetch the rope over and over and over again. When she was ready, she got Billy Joe to throw one of her dad's holey old leather gloves down next to the bit of rope and told Inca to fetch. Inca sniffed both glove and rope and chose the rope. He brought it back over the jump, sat, and dropped it at Ivy's feet.

"Bet he won't do it with all these old toys and socks," said Billy Joe.

"Bet he will," said Ivy. She knew it didn't matter how many pieces of junk were on the ground. Inca would only pick up the one with her smell. Dogs' noses were so good they could detect their person's particular smell from a great distance.

In an instant Inca picked up the rope again. This made Billy Joe go and cut up a whole length of clothesline into identical pieces. He spread them on the ground and mixed in the Ivy one near the middle.

"Try *that!*" he said.

Ivy smiled. She sent Inca over his hurdle. In one second he grabbed the right rope and brought it back.

Billy Joe didn't have a chance to say anything to that, because his mother's voice rang out like a dinner bell from the kitchen.

"Billy Joe!" she called. "You get my oven scrubbed out yet?"

A couple of days later, when Inca was a full three months old, a manila envelope came in the mail for Ivy from Mr. Burgess in New Jersey. It contained a dog ticket for American Airlines to fly

Inca to Newark, New Jersey, on the last Monday in August—just three days away! In a small silver wrapper was a tranquilizer pill, so Inca would sleep the whole journey. Also enclosed was another ten-dollar bill for Ivy's dad, to pay for his trouble.

"Ain't trouble," said Ivy's father. "Put it in the envelope, honey. You got college to pay for. Don't let that boy know a thing about it, either."

Inca was not a perfect dog. He liked to crawl on his belly, an inch at a time, toward the supper table when the guests were eating. No amount of *leave it*s or *down stay*s stopped him from begging ever so gently at the table and staring with false starving expressions at the guests. Ivy's mom made the decision to keep Inca in a horse stall at supper time so he would not bother anyone. Inca howled from the stable because he could smell supper cooking in the kitchen across the way.

It was over a last bite of a chicken wing that Ivy noticed an unusual silence. She excused herself from the table and ran out to the stable to see if Inca was doing all right in his stall. Her heart fell exactly as fast as a roller-coaster car when she saw the stall door open and no Inca inside.

She ran to the Butterworths' front door. "Where's Inca?" she shouted at Billy Joe.

"He'll come back," said Billy Joe. "I just hated seeing him all confined like a jailbird."

Ivy drew breath, narrowed her eyes, and swore at Billy Joe so no one but he could hear. "He's *my* dog. He's *my* responsibility, and you let him out into the night, you birdbrain!" she said.

Jim Butterworth came to the door and stood behind Billy Joe.

"He let Inca out," explained Ivy. "He's out there with coyotes and bears and I don't know what-all."

"Son, why'd you do that?" asked his father.

" 'Cause I didn't want to see him all cooped

up," whined Billy Joe. "I just meant for a minute. Then he . . . saw something, and . . . and he'll come on back. Dogs always come back. Look at Hoover and Coover. They're right here on the porch."

"He's not your dog to let out or let in. He belongs to that Burgess fellow, who paid a hundred dollars for him," said Mr. Butterworth. "And if he's not back here by airplane time Monday morning, you're going to have an awful lot of fence posts to paint and a winter's worth of bob wire to string, so you get your sorry rear end out there and find him. Y'hear?"

Ivy grabbed the best flashlight she could find in the barn. She swept its weak beam over the paddock and the hill beyond, and began a circle around the property. Billy Joe did the same thing, farther up the mountain.

"Inca! Inca, come!" they both called, again and again. But there was no Inca.

Owls hooted in the night wind. Coyotes yipped. Skunks, raccoons, mule deer, and other creatures padded and whisked through the scrub and sagebrush, invisible to Ivy, with her small flashlight.

At midnight, her mother made Ivy come back in, and despite her determination not to fall asleep, she drifted off at four in the morning in an armchair, none the hungrier for having missed half her dinner.

Ivy woke at six, the full light of the sun creeping in and then smacking her in the eyes where she sat, half-folded into the chair. She sat upright.

"Where am I?" Ivy asked herself, and then she remembered. It was Saturday morning. Her mother and Cora Butterworth were long gone to Reno for market day. Her dad was this minute on the trail with a few hardy guests who wanted to see the sunrise over the mountains. Her mother had left the front door open in case Inca should make his way back to her. But there was no Inca.

Ivy leaped up. She swallowed a gulp of orange juice, which her mother had left out for her, and ran outside to begin her search again.

Ivy didn't have to wait long. In the distance, from back of one of the big foothills that surrounded the ranch, someone called her name.

"Ivy! Ivy, come and help me!"

Ivy ran. "I'm coming!" she shouted.

She saw him from fifty yards and ran toward him. Billy Joe was walking slowly, Inca in his arms. The puppy's mouth was open and filled with bleeding slashes and bloody foam. His eyes and face and chest were covered with foot-long spines.

"Porcupine got him!" said Billy Joe. "He's hurt real bad."

Inca's head and nose were swollen up so that Ivy would hardly have recognized him. She tried to pull one of the spines out from under Inca's eye, but it was pinned into the dog's flesh like a fishhook, and broke off in her hand.

Billy Joe panted and managed to say, "He couldn't walk because he's got the quills in his feet, from trying to rip them off his face."

Ivy ran back to the house to call Dr. Rinaldi. There was no answer. Then she remembered—Saturday morning was his surgery time. He wouldn't be able to answer the phone. "We gotta get him to Dr. Rinaldi's!" shouted Ivy.

"How?" asked Billy Joe. He was shaking with the effort of carrying a forty-pound dog off the mountain. "How we gonna get him to the vet? Tell me that! We got nobody to drive us. My pop's at the airport, dropping off guests. By the time he gets back, this dog'll be a goner."

Billy Joe was right. Ivy knew it. But then

they saw their answer. Parked halfway into the rear entrance of the barn was Mr. Butterworth's old pickup truck. Ivy hopped into the passenger seat, then Billy Joe passed Inca to her. Billy Joe climbed into the driver's seat and put his hands on the wheel. They were shaking so badly he couldn't even move the gearshift or turn the key in the ignition.

"Get out of that seat, Billie Joe," said Ivy. "You're not allowed to drive, anyway. You hold Inca!"

For the first time that Ivy could recall, Billy Joe did not argue with her. He was too shaken up. Instead, he slid across the front seat and held Inca steady while Ivy got behind the wheel. She had never driven a vehicle before. She made her hands stop trembling, forcing herself to concentrate.

"Okay," Billy Joe said. "Turn the key. Right. Put your foot on that left-hand pedal. That's the clutch. Put the truck in reverse. Let the clutch out

easy and put a little pressure on the gas. When you get to the road, back it around and shift up to where it says three. That's third. Drive all the way in third gear so you don't have to shift."

That's exactly what Ivy did. They wheeled out onto the highway and drove the truck at forty miles an hour into town. If it took four hours or ten minutes, Ivy didn't know. She just knew that she began to breathe again when she saw the sign for Carson City Animal Hospital and turned into the vet's driveway.

"Let the clutch out now!" said Billy Joe. "Ease off that gas pedal. Right foot on the brake. Left foot back on the clutch. Pull that gearshift into neutral. Put your foot slow on the brake!"

There were tears of effort in Ivy's eyes, and she nearly bit through her lip with concentration. The truck stopped with a terrible metallic shudder and screech. By accident, Ivy hit the horn. The horn stuck and wouldn't stop blasting.

Inside of a confused minute full of shouts and door slammings, Inca was in Dr. Rinaldi's arms.

The vet shot Inca full of anesthetic and morphine while his nurse connected a fluid feed into his front leg. For the next hour and a half, Dr. Rinaldi, Ivy, and Billy Joe carefully unhooked each one of a hundred and sixty-five needle-sharp porcupine quills from Inca's ears, face, and chest.

By evening, only the little shaved square on Inca's front leg where the intravenous needle had gone in gave a clue that anything bad had happened to the puppy at all. Once the anesthetic wore off, he was bouncing around the way he always did.

At seven o'clock Monday morning, Inca swallowed a square of Velveeta cheese with the tranquilizer in it and kissed everybody good-bye a dozen times. Ivy closed up his hard-sided

127

carrier with the water bottle full and in place, and gave him over to the nice man with a crew cut in the American Airlines uniform.

"Good-bye, my Inca," she said shakily, and opened the crate door to once more hold his head and kiss his ears.

The man with the crew cut put the crate on a dolly and wheeled Inca away.

At eleven o'clock that night, the telephone rang. It was a telegram from Teaneck, New Jersey. The Western Union lady read it aloud to Ivy's dad, who then asked her to repeat the message to Ivy.

"Wife is gone (stop) but Inca is here (stop) Very happy (stop) Thanks (stop) Burgess (stop) Gift follows (stop)."

The gift was for Ivy. It came on September first in a green box with GERMAN SHEPHERD CLUB OF AMERICA stamped in gold on the lid. Inside was a Timex watch. Pictured on its face was a black-and-tan shepherd head, just like Inca's. *You'll need this if you are to run a business, girl!* read the card. *Best wishes, George Burgess.*

That night, Ivy kept a hand on Inca's empty crate. Annie would be back in two days. School would begin in five. She realized that she missed Inca much more than she had missed Annie. With a dog, there was no guessing as to who loved whom in the world. There were no embarrassments or shifting loyalties. Ivy kept her feelings silent in case Billy Joe could hear through her window. But Ivy's mother knew. She came in and sat on the edge of Ivy's bed. "We'll find you a pup at the pound, honey."

But Ivy didn't want a pup from the pound. She wanted Inca. She knew that disappointment was a part of life. You couldn't always get what you wanted. But, oh, she wanted that Inca.

Ivy lay on her bed with her hands folded under her chin. She listened to the night sounds: the tree frogs and cheeping cicadas mixing their voices with Cora Butterworth's, talking on the phone to her sister through the late-summer night.

★ ★ ★

In the morning, Ivy overheard Billy Joe in conversation with his mother.

"Let me read you this, son," Billy Joe's mother said. "'Dear Mrs. Butterworth, I know how hard it is to pay for the medicines we use to save animals' lives. I am going to forgo all charges for the recent porcupine incident. But it would be nice if I could have a few hours of help cleaning up the premises here at the animal hospital at the end of the day. Sincerely, Bob Rinaldi.' Every day till Christmas, Billy Joe," said his mother.

"That'll learn you to be careful of other people's property."

Hearing this through her window, Ivy smiled for the first time since Inca had left. She knew no list of chores was going to teach Billy Joe Butterworth a thing he didn't want to know, but Billy Joe wasn't all bad. He'd stayed out all that terrible night looking for Inca. He'd found Inca and carried him for miles off that mountain. So she figured she'd pitch in and help Billy Joe at Dr. Rinaldi's. Taking care of animals wasn't her idea of hard work. And who knew where it might lead?

Andromeda

Ivy," Annie warned her in a whisper. "Don't wear that new dog watch of yours in school. Leave it here in your locker. Wear it at home but not in front of you-know-who."

"Why not?" Ivy asked.

Annie squirmed uncomfortably in front of their newly assigned hall lockers. "Because . . ." Annie started. "Just because it looks like a boy's watch. It isn't a stylish watch at all. And certain people are going to notice."

"Who?" asked Ivy.

"You know perfectly well who," snapped Annie. "Take it off, Ivy. I don't want to spend the whole year with MLM and her friends iceberging us."

But Ivy did not take off her Inca watch. Later, as they were filing into the lunchroom, Mary Louise Merriweather shook her blond curls dizzily and presented every girl with a challenge. Who could get a Star Crazy watch like hers and wear it to school the next day? Would all the different-colored jewels and wristbands make it into the sixth grade?

"Those Star Crazies are the fakest things I've ever seen!" Ivy said to Annie as they unpacked their lunches.

"Shhhh," said Annie quickly. "MLM is listening."

And so she was. Mary Louise sauntered by on the way to her popular girls' lunch table. "Got a new watch, hunh, Ivy? Look at that. A dog! Isn't that cute. Look, girls!"

"You shouldn't have said anything, Ivy," Annie scolded. "Now it's too late."

"Too late?" Ivy asked. "Too late for what?" But Ivy knew. Mary Louise could create a little warm heaven for whomever she blessed and she could just as quickly assign you to Siberia. Ivy was now in Siberia, and Annie didn't want to be there with her.

Mary Louise's best friend, Jennifer, strolled over to the table where Annie and Ivy were eating. "Hey, Annie Evans!" said Jennifer sweetly, "Come and see this!"

Annie stood. "I told you you should have taken the dog watch off," she whispered, and wrapping up the second half of her sandwich, Annie followed Jennifer to the popular girls' lunch table.

As easily as being snatched into the doors of

a flying saucer, Annie walked up the ladder that had been extended down to her and entered Mary Louise heaven.

It was no good telling anybody about this. Ivy's mom and dad would just sigh and say Annie would soon forget about whatever foolishness went on at school and be herself again. Ivy knew this was not going to happen.

Fridays were paydays for Ivy. She got a silver dollar a week from Dr. Rinaldi for her assistance at his clinic. Sometimes in the evening, Ivy clinked the big dollar coins out of their envelope and counted them out on the table. Her mother found her doing this one night after supper.

"Penny for your thoughts, honey," she had said.

"Just counting," said Ivy.

"We don't see Annie," said her mother. "We haven't seen her since school began."

"Annie," said Ivy, "is taking Eastern show-riding lessons three times a week in Reno. Her mother drives her. There's some indoor ring there with jumps and hedges and stuff. I think she got into it at camp this summer. They do English riding and show jumping there." Ivy said nothing about Annie's new friends.

Her mother sniffed and cast around her chair for her sewing box. "That kind of horse show business'll run you into the poor house sooner than a one-arm bandit," she said, taking out a sock that needed darning, holding its ragged toe up to the light, and inserting the darning egg. "Of course, Annie's people don't have to worry about such things as money."

Annie had been invited to sit at lunch permanently with Mary Louise and her gang. Each day Ivy watched her friend breathe in the Mary Louise laughing gas and then, after school was over, quickly disappear into another world. Ivy was too shy to ask Annie if the tourmaline ring ever made it in the mail to Camp Allegro.

Ivy rode alone to the animal hospital after school. Without a bike of his own, Billy Joe had managed only three work days in September and October combined to pay off his debt to Dr. Rinaldi. In the end, Cora Butterworth paid up Inca's bill, because the trouble of driving Billy Joe to work and fetching him again wasn't worth it.

But Ivy never stopped going. At the vet's, Ivy cleaned up the dog runs and the cat boxes. She fed the animals, watered them, and exercised the ones that needed it. She liked the work. She was allowed to take temperatures, remove stitches with a tiny pliers, and change IV bottles.

Dr. Rinaldi had promised that in a month's time, she could assist at a spaying surgery.

One day in November, Ivy stopped at Dr. Rinaldi's examining room before she left the vet's building. Someone's collie was on the table, whimpering about an ear examination. Ivy hopped up to sit on the table and took the dog's head in her hands, holding him steady for the otoscope.

Dr. Rinaldi asked her, "Ivy, did you ever hear of the Mexican Derby at the Agua Caliente track down in Tijuana?"

"I've heard of the Agua Caliente track," said Ivy. She loved all things horse and so read the track news in the sports pages of the *Reno Gazette Journal*.

"Filly named Andromeda beat the big

champion, Seabiscuit, by four lengths at Agua Caliente some years back. That's the race they call the Mexican Derby. Not quite Santa Anita or the Preakness, but it's a big race all the same."

"Seabiscuit! He's the most famous horse since Man o' War!" said Ivy. "Seabiscuit was famous before I could read the papers!"

"Well, Andromeda beat him by three lengths. She was going to be the best filly champion of all time," said Dr. Rinaldi.

"What happened to Andromeda?" asked Ivy, supposing this story might not have such a happy ending.

"Apparently she stumbled at the finish line in her next race. Threw her jockey and nearly killed him. She got a bowed tendon. Had to quit the track."

"Can a bowed tendon be fixed?" asked Ivy.

Dr. Rinaldi squirted yellow ointment into

the collie's ear. The dog shook her head violently, spraying ointment all over Ivy and the vet.

He answered, squirting more ointment into the other ear. "Sometimes the leg comes back healthy. Sometimes not. Now she's too old to race again. That leg'll always be a little hinky."

"How do you know all about this, Dr. Rinaldi?" asked Ivy, massaging the base of the collie's ears so that the medicine would spread out inside.

"A few years ago, family named Montgomery out at Spooner Lake found her at an auction. The Montgomerys buy down-and-out off-track horses, and she sure was down-and-out. They bought Andromeda. She's fine now!" Dr. Rinaldi added. "She's my patient."

"I'm glad for her," said Ivy. She hated animal stories that ended badly. "What happened to the jockey?"

"She came with him," said Dr. Rinaldi. "Name is Ruben Velez. After he got out of the hospital, he followed Andromeda. Auction to auction. Wherever she lived, he lived. But Ruben needs a little help from time to time. The Montgomerys called me up last night. They have to go east for a while. Their daughter's baby is being born. I recommended you to help Ruben out with their five pasture horses, Ivy. Interested?"

"Can't Ruben see to the pasture horses?" asked Ivy.

"Well, they need water and hay."

"But what about Ruben? Can't he do that?" asked Ivy.

"Ruben has another job that takes him from the farm for a good chunk of the evenings. He's also blind."

"Blind!"

"He lost his helmet in that race and a couple

of horses stepped on his head. He's lucky to be alive."

Ivy held the trembling collie's head under her arm and made clucking noises to calm him. "Can Ruben walk and all? Is he in a wheelchair?" she asked.

"He's fine," said Dr. Rinaldi. "In the day Ruben cares for Andromeda, but then he takes the bus to his night job at the old folks' home."

"Does Ruben still ride?"

"Oh, yes. He says Andromeda is like a mother to him."

"Spooner Lake," said Ivy. "That's way off west of here. It's ten miles or more on Old Creek Road. It'll be dark by the time I get there. I don't think my folks'd let me bike it."

"Yes, but there's a school-bus route out there. On weekends if you rode over on horseback instead of biking, you could go over the mountain and shortcut it," said Dr. Rinaldi. "The holiday season ain't the divorce season. You got Mirabel and Texas and that old paint mare just standin' around eating hay. You could get over to Spooner Lake on Mirabel in no time if you cut across Mule Canyon."

Ivy had to agree. The Mule Canyon trail was her dad's favorite guest ride. Even the Never-Been-on-a-Horse-Befores could manage it.

"Not only that," said Dr. Rinaldi. "The Montgomerys'll pay a buck a day. Good money for your vet-school savings, if you ask me. More'n I can pay you!"

"What would they want me to do?" asked Ivy.

"You gotta throw five flakes of hay into the pasture every day and make sure the horse water in their trough isn't frozen. Rabbits need feed and water. Barn cat, too. Chickens need their feed, and their eggs collected. Lot of busy work."

"Dollar a day? I'll do it," said Ivy.

Ivy presented the Montgomerys' request to her parents after the supper dishes were done, when they were in good moods.

"Honey," said Ivy's dad, "you can take Mirabel over the mountain, no problem, but we don't want you going alone as far as Spooner Lake."

Her mother added, "It's dark at four o'clock nowadays. You gotta go in the early morning, and you gotta have company on that ride over the mountains."

Ivy knew who the company would have to be. She didn't want to go over the mountain with Billy Joe. She didn't want to share her pay with Billy Joe, who was sure to demand half her salary. She would have to say no to the Montgomerys.

"But Ivy, you come so well recommended by Dr. Rinaldi," said Mrs. Montgomery encouragingly on the telephone. "How about this? Weekdays after school, you could ride as far out as our place at Spooner Lake on the number-six school bus. The school bus goes right by our mailbox. After you feed and water the animals, you could catch a ride back to town with the mailman; he never gets out to our ranch much before five in the evening anyway. I'll speak to him and see if he can pick you up and bring you home on his way back to town each weekday. Then on the weekends, you can ride your horse back and forth in the daylight."

It was a deal after all. Weekdays Ivy would travel by school bus and mailman. Billy Joe and the trip across the mountains would be weekends only. Ivy figured she could pay Billy Joe fifty cents out of her dollar a day, two days a week. A dollar a week would keep him in bubble gum and fireworks for the four weekends required. She wished she had Inca for company instead of a troublemaking boy like Billy Joe.

"Don't think for one minute you're gonna get rich, Billy Joe," said Ivy. "I can only afford to pay you half my weekend salary, and you gotta help me, too."

But Billy Joe's eyes sparkled at the mention of Spooner Lake and Spooner Summit. "I have a secret plan!" said Billy Joe. "I bet you straight up I come out of this richer 'n you! I know something about that mountain east of Spooner Lake."

Ivy knew better than to ask what Billy Joe's harebrained secret plan was.

After school let out on her first Montgomery day, Ivy waited for the number-six bus to pull up and load its kids. A voice behind her piped up.

"Ivy! What are you doing on the six bus?"

It was Annie. She stood in the wind in full riding habit, shiny black paddock boots, fawn jodhpurs, and a velvet hard hat under her arm. The wind blew her tweed hacking jacket open for a moment, and Ivy could read the label on the silk lining: YOUNG RIDERS' CLUB. SAKS FIFTH AVENUE. NEW YORK.

"Oh, I'm working," said Ivy, "taking care of someone's horses out at Spooner Lake."

"Working!" said Annie. "You didn't tell me!"

"How could I have told you?" asked Ivy. "When?"

A cloud seemed to pass over Annie's eyes. But at that moment, her mother drew up in their car, scattering school-yard gravel underneath.

"Let's talk, Ivy!" said Annie. "I hate those girls!"

Ivy longed for Annie to explain who "those girls" were, but there was no time. Annie tossed her hard hat onto the backseat, onto a pile of mail, and jumped into the car.

Ivy could smell Annie's mother's perfume as

the car door stood open. She knew it as well as the smell of her own kitchen.

"Dear!" said Annie's mother. "We're all going to Colorado to ski the day after Christmas. Won't you come along? We have an extra ticket!"

Ivy hesitated. She wanted this badly. But she answered, "I have to work. I'm taking care of some horses out near Spooner Lake."

"But surely . . ." began Annie's mother.

"Couldn't Billy Joe take over for you? Come on, Ivy," said Annie.

Again Ivy hesitated. *Why did I take this job?* she asked herself angrily. But there was no getting around it. "Billy Joe is not responsible," she answered in a small voice. "It's . . . I'll make thirty dollars toward college, and I can't get out of it."

In Annie's eyes and in her mother's was the flicker of recognition of another world. One they would never touch, just as Ivy would never touch the world of Camp Allegro. Ivy's was the world of carefully marked money envelopes. Ivy wished she could take both Annie's and her mother's hands in hers and reverse time to last year, but only a cheerful "Another time, then! We're late!" rang out from the familiar bright-red lips and white teeth. Then Annie and her mother waved good-bye.

Ivy took a seat by a window on the number-six bus. She watched Mrs. Evans's taillights disappear north on the highway to Reno. Would Annie ask that tent mate instead? Was there really an extra ticket on an airplane to Colorado? There was no way of knowing. Maybe Annie had a whole bevy of new friends at the Reno riding place. There had been mail on the backseat of the car where Annie's helmet was tossed. Ivy had only a second to see a mess of forms with a familiar emblem on the pages: a hand holding a lamp. That emblem held an answer, Ivy knew suddenly. She had seen that hand and lamp emblem somewhere, but just where, Ivy could not put her finger.

Spooner Lake was half an hour by bus from the school. The Montgomery place was the last stop before the bus turned around. To a visitor the ranch looked tiny against the huge landscape of pastures and mountains surrounding it. Ivy walked down the frozen muddy driveway and held out her hand to the five horses who gathered along the fence. A man appeared then, in the stable doorway.

Ivy went up to him. "Hi, I'm Ivy," she said. "You must be Mr. Velez!" Ivy had never met a blind person in her life.

"Ruben," he answered. He extended his hand. "This here's my horse, Andromeda," he said, indicating the occupant of the stall behind him. "Where she goes, I go."

Ruben stood an inch shorter than Ivy. He scooted around the stable like a small chef in a big kitchen. He knew exactly where he was in the stable at all times and just what he was doing. Ruben showed Ivy the ropes in no time.

"Andromeda don't go out in the pasture with the othern," he explained to Ivy. "She could turn an ankle in a gopher hole. Wind's too cold for her. Anything can happen to a Thoroughbred racer, and usually it does happen. You like horses?"

"I love them. All animals," said Ivy.

Andromeda stood patiently on her cross ties. Ruben had two brushes in his hand—a stiff one and a finishing brush.

"Put your hand on her," Ruben instructed Ivy. "Right on the withers. That's it. Now take this brush and give her coat a good once-over."

Ivy did. Andromeda's coat gleamed under her hand.

"She liked that," said Ruben. "She likes your hands. Do you know how to ride?"

"All my life," said Ivy. "But I only ride trail ponies. I've never been on a big horse like this one."

"Oh, Andromeda's like an old rocking chair," said Ruben. "Next time I take her out, I'll let you ride. Would you like that?"

"I'd love it," said Ivy.

"I have to go to work in a few minutes. You all right here alone?" asked Ruben.

"I'm fine," said Ivy.

Ruben removed his boots and put his feet into black city shoes. "I take care of the old," he said. "Most of 'em can't see me, and I can't see them, but it don't matter. I love them. When I come in the ward, they all know. They love my stories. I tell them all the stories from the track in the old days."

Ruben had prepared Andromeda's dinner

beforehand. She got hay and some sweet feed. Her water bucket was full.

"It's ten to four," he said. "You mind feeding her? The bus will be here soon, so I have to go." Ivy heard no clock or chime. How did Ruben know the time?

Before he left the stable, Ruben turned to Ivy with a mischievous smile. "I have a clock in my head," he said.

Ivy handed a carrot to Andromeda, who took the treat in her velvet lips, as gently as a baby.

There was no water in the stable pipes, so Ivy had to pump the horses' water into two buckets at an outdoor pump. She carried it to the pasture and sloshed it, bucket by bucket, into the old bathtub that was the water trough. Before pouring new water, she had to break up any ice that had formed. She pitchforked the ice pieces out onto the grass. The bathtub took an easy twenty buckets, but she stopped at ten.

After the watering, Ivy climbed into the hay-
loft and kicked a new hay bale down on the
stable floor with a thump. She put five big flakes
of hay into a wheelbarrow and wheeled it out
to the near pasture, where the horses were waiting for her. Then she fed the rabbits and cleaned
their cage, and scattered handfuls of cracked corn
in the chicken yard, where there were a dozen
Rhode Island Red hens. Ivy collected the day's
eggs in a small basket.

Ivy's last chores were sweeping the barn,
wheeling out Andromeda's old bedding, forking it into the manure pile, then feeding and
watering the barn cat, Striper. She made sure
Andromeda needed nothing.

Most days that followed were just the same.
Ivy could only fit in a short half hour in the paddock on Andromeda's back, with Ruben leading
her, before the dark came and Ruben had to
catch the bus to his job. Ruben knew exactly

where Ivy was, and exactly where the horse was, as if he could see.

"You are a good rider," said Ruben. "I can hear it and feel it."

Each night Ivy said good night to Andromeda before switching off the lights and closing the stable door. Carrying her book bag, Ivy whistled as she walked down the drive to the mailboxes. There she waited in the night wind to flag down the mail carrier on his last run of the day. Ivy worried that the mailman wouldn't linger if she wasn't out there promptly.

Weekends meant going over the mountain, Ivy on Mirabel and Billy Joe on Texas.

"I am going to make a fortune on Spooner Summit," Billy Joe crowed to her on their first morning out.

Ivy was tempted to call Billy Joe a birdbrain,

but she didn't, because he would start on back calling her Miss Climbing Vine.

Ivy did notice that on one side of Texas's saddle, Billy Joe had strapped a big ax and a shovel and on the other side, a large empty leather bag from the woodpile.

"What's that ax for?" Ivy asked him while they saddled up for the trip.

"That's a state secret!" said Billy Joe.

On Saturdays and Sundays, Ruben gave Andromeda her full workout. This included a walk, a trot, and a canter on the flat and sandy trail that ran around the Montgomery ranch. But before Ruben allowed Andromeda to set a hoof on it, he had Ivy check the entire track. How fast Andromeda could go was something that Ivy would likely never know.

"Take that trail horse of yourn," said Ruben.

"Ride around this half-mile track. Use your sharp little eyes and make sure there's no new holes to trip up our girl."

A mild Saturday came, and Ruben decided he would let Ivy ride one circuit at a trot on his precious Andromeda's back. Every moment Ivy sat up on the big, graceful horse felt like a moment in another world. While trotting her perfectly around the well-inspected half mile took only two minutes, she knew those two minutes would stay with her a long time.

Riding Thoroughbreds is Annie's life now, Ivy reminded herself, dismounting and giving the reins to Ruben. Annie gets to do this three times a week and go over jumps, too, with that hard hat and those boots. Ivy had found the price of Annie's paddock boots in one of the Montgomerys' tack-room catalogs. They cost more than all the silver dollars in her university envelope.

Billy Joe leaned on the paddock fence and watched. He chewed his bubble gum slowly and snapped it loudly.

"She don't like your chewing gum, boy," said Ruben to Billy Joe. "See how she steps to the side when you're in the picture? She don't like that snapping noise you make."

"I've been riding horses just as long as Ivy here," Billy Joe argued.

"Yeah, but this one don't want you near her," said Ruben, "not with that gum smell on you. Makes her nervous."

When Ruben was out of earshot, Ivy turned to Billy Joe, both of them leaning up on the fence, watching Ruben canter in a perfect oval.

"Billy Joe," said Ivy patiently, "you want to get up on this filly, don't you?"

"Never said that," said Billy Joe.

"I know you, Billy Joe," Ivy said. "You want to tell the guys at school you went a flat mile

161

on the horse that beat Seabiscuit. Well, Ruben won't let you, and that's that."

"I've got better things to do," said Billy Joe. He blew an enormous pink bubble and popped it with his finger.

Three Saturday mornings in a row, Billy Joe jumped on Texas's back and mysteriously disappeared up into the mountain that lay just to the east of Spooner Lake. His ax and shovel and leather bag dangled from the saddle. Every time, he came back empty-handed and never said what he'd been doing.

Ivy warned Billy Joe to be back at the stable in time to break up the bathtub ice or she wouldn't pay him his fifty cents. "You come late and you pay for it," she warned him.

"Surprise of the world!" he said with a big grin, each time he returned from his mountain wanderings.

Andromeda was a huge mass of horse muscle

on four delicate racer's legs. Ivy and Billy Joe were used to quarter horses, strong all the way up and down. Andromeda's value and her precious race horse legs kept even Billy Joe on his toes.

After her exercise, Ivy and Ruben cross-tied Andromeda in the stable across from her stall. Ivy removed the saddle and let the saddle blanket dry separately, everything on its own rack or peg. The bridle had to be cleaned with leather cleaner and the bit soaked in soapy water. Ruben made Billy Joe spit out his gum and wash out his mouth before he was allowed in the stable to help dry Andromeda after her hot walk. There was no washing Andromeda in the cold weather. That was an invite to trouble.

"You know what'll happen if we mess up anything with their horses," whispered Ivy. "I'll lose my good name and never get another job, and your mother and father will kill you."

One night, Ruben told Ivy to look up on the tack room wall behind where the halters hung. Thumbtacked to the wall were faded news clippings and photos of the triumphant race against Seabiscuit at the Agua Caliente track.

"Would you read 'em to me?" Ruben asked.

"'Andromeda,'" Ivy began, "'a filly from Intermountain Stables in West Texas, triumphed over racing's biggest star today . . .'"

She read all three of the newspaper accounts of Andromeda's great victory. Each one mentioned Ruben by name.

"Again," said Ruben when she had finished.

★   ★   ★

"Look what I found!" crowed Billy Joe one morning. It was the Saturday after Thanksgiving, and

he'd been poking around in the Montgomerys'
tack room. He came out holding Andromeda's
little racing saddle from her winner's circle days.
Above its rack hung the helmet with the blue
and white Intermountain Stable colors that
Ruben had worn in the Mexican Derby on
the day Andromeda'd been covered with glory.
Billy Joe lifted the little saddle up in one hand.
"Doesn't weigh a thing," he said.

Ruben cocked his head. "Three pounds," he
said. "That's as light as they can make 'em and
still have the saddle hold up during the race."

"Do you miss it awful bad?" asked Billy Joe.

"Racing," Ruben said, "is a cruel and terrible
thing to do to a beautiful animal. All the same,
sitting on that horse's back, flyin' like the wind
itself, and winning. . . . That's what I miss. Until
you do it, you don't know. It's like the stars up
close. It's not a wonder I'm blind." He put his

hand to his eyes. "Put that gear back where you found it, boy," Ruben said, and added, "I wouldn't want a spot on it."

Billy Joe put the saddle neatly back on its rack under Ruben's old silks in the tack-room closet. As soon as his chores were done, Billy Joe left for his mysterious mission on Spooner Summit.

One day in December, as he took off on Texas's back, Ivy said, "I'll bet I know what you're after, Billy Joe. You're looking for that old silver mine they closed up when Virginia City went broke."

Billy Joe just smiled and gave Texas a little flap on the neck with his reins to speed him up the mountain.

Ivy could not figure out why Billy Joe would go hunting for an old mine in the cold of winter. And if he were, he'd need just a shovel, not an ax.

* ★ ★ ★ *

The day school closed for Christmas break, Ivy rode the bus, as always, out to the last stop.

On foot she led Andromeda on her usual walk around the paddock. Tumbleweed skittered in big tangled balls across the paddock. Ruben waited in the stable door because the wind hurt his eyes. Still, he "watched" in his own way. Ivy gave Andromeda no more than twenty minutes of exercise, so she wouldn't get all sweated up in the late December wind. According to *The Home Vet,* the slightest chill could cause a race horse's muscles to go into spasm. There was always something to look for: colic, muscle spasms, heaves, dark urine. You name it, they got it.

"You're a big baby," she said to the filly when she brought her in. Ruben's hand waited in the air, at just the right level to grasp the bridle while

Ivy dismounted. Then he tucked Andromeda away for the night.

"Now I must go to take care of my *abuelos* and *abuelas,*" Ruben said. "My grandpas and grandmamas."

As always, Ruben got his bus exactly on time.

Snow had been forecast for that evening. Ivy gave the paddock horses extra hay. She broke up a big clot of ice in their tub and refilled it. The cat got an extra piece of chicken breast Ivy had saved from her lunch. The bunnies got carrots and half a head of lettuce too old for Ivy's mother to keep.

Ivy checked everything twice to make sure that, big and little, the details were covered in the stable. Then she slung her book bag onto her back, went out to the highway, and waited by the mailbox for the mail truck to come by and pick her up. She stamped her feet in the cold and watched as the dark gathered over the mountains and blacked out everything in the valley.

Ivy spotted the mail truck's familiar head-lights rising a mile down Old Creek Road. Out of habit, she turned to double-check that every-thing was right at the Montgomery stable and saw a light blink on!

Heart pumping, Ivy ran back up the drive. This meant she would surely miss her ride. The mailman only pulled up if he saw her standing on the road. She would have to call her father to come get her, which he didn't like doing. But she had no choice. There was no question that someone was in the stable with Andromeda.

Ivy reached the stable. Winded, she threw open the stable door, and peered in. Someone called her name, and there stood Billy Joe Butterworth, looking for all heaven like he'd just seen a ghost.

"Billy Joe, what are you doing here on a

Friday?" asked Ivy, her breath coming hard in steamy clouds on the dark winter air. "You made me miss my ride home!"

"Ivy," Billy Joe gasped. "I've got big trouble. Get a flashlight!"

Ivy grabbed a flashlight and followed Billy Joe into the night. He raced ahead of her, up and up a twisting path onto Spooner Summit.

The path was nearly invisible in the moonless dark. It wound around and over rock outcroppings, chinquapin bushes, and spiky scrub cedars that could rip the shirt off your back. About half a mile up the trail, Billy Joe stopped at a clearing. He looked right and left, getting his bearings in the dark and looking for something. Ivy flashed her light from tree to tree. Then she saw Billy Joe's horse, Texas, leaning against a live oak, breath coming hard. Billy Joe unwound his reins from a low limb where he'd tied him. Ivy went up to Texas and shone the light up and down his head. A gasping noise came out of the horse's mouth. His face looked weirdly heavy.

"What happened?" asked Ivy.

"Snakebite! Rattler!" said Billy Joe. "He put his nose down and the snake just bit him. I killed it."

"Rattler?" said Ivy. "Billy Joe, there's no rattlers out in December. They don't come out until spring, when it warms up."

"This one did!" said Billy Joe.

Beneath a twisted manzanita stump by the trailside writhed the beheaded body of a six-foot diamondback rattlesnake. It was half alive, whipping back and forth in the night. A big drop of sweat ran down Ivy's backbone. Snakes were the only critters she didn't like, and she really didn't like them at all.

Texas's face had swelled up to twice its

usual size. "Cut the bridle off him. He's gonna suffocate," said Ivy. Billy Joe got out his knife and sliced through Texas' noseband.

"Now hold this flashlight," Ivy said. She put her hands on either side of Texas's head and listened carefully to his breathing. "He's having trouble getting air. Let's get him down to the Montgomerys' stable. He's gonna need a shot of antivenom, fast. We'll have to call Dr. Rinaldi."

They led Texas slowly down the trail, Billy Joe carrying Texas's saddle so there was less weight on the exhausted horse. Holding her flashlight, Ivy guided Billy Joe and Texas away from the snake, down the curling path. The horse seemed not to know what was happening or where he was. Texas snorted, pulling air through his mouth. He went slower and slower, stumbling on the loose, stony path, unable to see or breathe.

"Soon as we see the light of the stable, I'll run ahead to the house and the phone," said

Ivy. "Do you think you can get him into the spare stall?"

"I'll try," said Billy Joe.

As soon as the stable light came into view at the end of the trail, Ivy gave the flashlight to Billy Joe and sprinted like a deer toward the dark house. Freezing hands shaking, she fumbled for the key to the main house, then let herself in. She prayed the Montgomerys were not on a six-family party line, but the phone was not busy.

Dr. Rinaldi had just left his office. Irma, his secretary, said she'd see if she could flag him down in the parking lot. Time ticked by on the Inca watch, second by second. Finally, Dr. Rinaldi came on the line.

"Ivy, what's wrong?"

"I'm out at the Montgomery place," she said. "Billy Joe's horse, Texas, has been bit on the nose by a rattler."

"In winter?" said Dr. Rinaldi. "Are you sure?"

"Believe me, I saw 'im. A six-footer, right on the trail," said Ivy.

"Okay, but it'll take me twenty minutes to get there," said Dr. Rinaldi with a sigh. "In the meantime, the horse's airway could become blocked completely by the swelling. I need you to go into the tack room, Ivy. Get the stable hose out. Take a shears. You'll find one somewhere in that big drawer. Cut two nine-inch lengths of hose. Jam 'em into the horse's nostrils to open his airway until I can get there. Don't worry that the hose is too big—a horse has big nasal tubes to the lungs. You've got to really push the hose up. D'ya hear?"

"I hear."

"Can you do it?"

"I'll try."

"That's my girl!"

After he hung up and the empty telephone line buzzed in her ear, Ivy felt keenly alone.

In the stable, Billy Joe had led Texas into an empty stall next to Andromeda's. Texas's front legs buckled. Slowly, the horse slid down the side of the stall and lay on the floor. Next door, Andromeda stamped and whinnied.

"Spit that gum out, Billy Joe," shouted Ivy. "Your chewing and snapping make Andromeda nervous. You know that." Ivy's fingers fumbled on the freezing hose. It took long minutes to find the shears. Then she found she didn't have the strength to cut through the reinforced rubber.

"Billy Joe, can you cut me two nine-inch lengths of this hose?" said Ivy. "Your hands are stronger."

Billy Joe had to put the heel of his boot on the shears to get the blades to cut through the stiff, frozen rubber. He swore. Ivy ignored him. She had a terrible certainty that he had somehow invited this snake trouble, but this was no time to ask.

The swelling on Texas's face increased by the minute. His head was a deformed thing in Ivy's hands, like a nightmare horse from some Greek myth she'd seen in a book.

"Easy, boy," Ivy said. "Easy."

The horse tried to lift his head.

"Hold his neck, now," said Ivy. Billy Joe stretched his body over the horse's neck and face so she'd have a clear shot at the nose. Ivy's hands barely managed to hold the end of the dirty green hose. With one push, she inserted it deep into his right nostril. Then she pushed the other one into the left side. Texas lifted his head. His eyes were glassy and, as quickly as he had looked up, his head dropped back onto the cold floor. But he could breathe again. He snorted air into his lungs in deep drafts that burbled as the air went up the artificial openings.

Billy Joe took off his wool jacket and tucked it under Texas's head. If the horse was a little more comfortable, he didn't show it. His big body twitched and shook from cold and shock.

"About ten more minutes now," said Ivy, checking her watch.

Billy Joe's face was as white as a candle. His eyes, fierce, scanned the bit of road visible through the stable window. If there was a beam that he and Ivy could have sent to Dr. Rinaldi to get him there one minute faster, they would have used it.

Texas was quiet now, yet Andromeda still fidgeted. It was well known that horses didn't like the smell of snakes, but the snake was far behind them, back up on the trail.

Ivy rubbed Texas's neck and whispered a chatter of little sounds into his ears to reassure him, and maybe reassure Andromeda, too. A cat stretched on the cobwebby windowsill, then turned and leaped down to visit them. Ivy breathed the cold and dusty stable air in and out, in and out, and listened that Texas was breathing, too. Her knees froze on the stone floor next to him. She didn't care. Andromeda still stamped and huffed.

Billy Joe had pitched Texas's saddle and blanket into the corner of the stable. Ivy noticed with mild interest that the leather saddlebag lay awkwardly beneath the blanket but that the ever-present ax and shovel were missing. Ivy's focus then shifted back to the road outside, and she willed Dr. Rinaldi's truck to turn the corner and fill their anxious darkness with the light of his kindly hands and voice.

Out of the corner of her eye, she thought she saw the leather saddlebag move. *I must be tired,* she thought. And then it moved again.

"Billy Joe, what is in that infernal saddlebag over there?" asked Ivy.

"Nothing's in it," Billy Joe's voice squeaked. "Leave it." He stood and went over to the corner where the blanket and bag lay.

Ivy spoke between her clenched teeth at Billy Joe. "There is something moving in that bag, Billy Joe, and you better tell me what it is, because Andromeda smells it and she's going to kick down her stall. I don't like this one bit, Billy Joe."

"You're imagining things is all," said Billy Joe. "If it makes you feel better, I'll go put the saddlebag outside."

But even Billy Joe was not prepared to have the leather bag buck and flip in his hands. Out of the saddlebag and onto the stable floor spilled a five-foot rattlesnake, its head not quite severed. The jaws spanned open and then snapped shut, again and again, while the body writhed.

Ivy screamed. Andromeda's hooves beat against her water bucket and feed crib.

"I thought it was dead!" Ivy shouted. "I saw it up there on the trail!"

"This is a different one!" said Billy Joe.

"Get the fire ax off the wall behind the tack room, Billy Joe!" she yelled. "Cut that snake's head off before it bites Texas again, or me or you or Andromeda!"

The rattler's body was as big around as a weight lifter's arm. It switched and levitated off the stable floor. Billy Joe backed away from it toward the tack room.

"Hurry up!" said Ivy. "Andromeda's going to break down her stall door any minute!"

Billy Joe hesitated. "I'm saving the skin!" he shouted. "You can get five bucks a dried skin from boot makers in Reno. If the head's attached, you get a buck more."

"*Your* head's not gonna be attached if that snake isn't dead in two seconds!" shouted Ivy. Still Billy Joe didn't move.

Andromeda butted the top hinge off her stall door.

Ivy sprang to her feet, closed Texas's stall door on the way, and grabbed the Montgomerys' rusty fire ax from the wall. She flew back, to within five feet of the snake, and brought the blade down flat on its snapping head. Then she slammed the sharp edge of the ax blade through its writhing vertebrae until it stopped moving.

"You wrecked the skin!" yelled Billy Joe.

"How can you talk about a stupid old snake-skin, Billy Joe, when your daddy's horse is about dying? That's what I'd like to know," said Ivy, tossing the ax in a corner. "Just wait and see how wrecked you are with your pop and mom if Texas doesn't make it."

Billy Joe stood with his hands in his pockets, looking completely stupid.

Ivy gave him a disgusted snort and went over to Andromeda's stall where she tried talking the

182

horse down. She brought her hand, full of sweet feed, under Andromeda's muzzle to distract her. Andromeda shook herself but stopped stamping and backing around her stall.

"What's going on?" Dr. Rinaldi stood in the doorway, sounding a little alarmed and taking in the scene—the big snake's body, still twitching slightly in the corner and the snake's head about a foot away.

Ivy lit up the instant she saw the vet, then looked at Billy Joe. Billy Joe looked so pathetic, Ivy could not bring herself to rat on him.

"Somehow," Ivy said to Dr. Rinaldi, "another snake got into the barn. Must have been asleep since summertime. We took care of it."

Dr. Rinaldi knelt at Texas's side. "Son, get down here and hold your horse's head steady while I inject the antivenom," he instructed Billy Joe.

Dr. Rinaldi prepared two large syringes. At

the sight of the needles, Billy Joe passed out, so it was Ivy who held Texas's head. Dr. Rinaldi eased the first shot into the horse's withers. Texas began to breathe better, his sides expanding and contracting like a moving mountain.

"Lucky I had enough antivenom this time of year," said Dr. Rinaldi. "Get the smelling salts out of the tack-room cupboard, Ivy, and hold 'em under that infernal boy's nose."

It wasn't long before Andromeda quieted in her stall and Texas began to try to stand up. "Needs another shot," said Dr. Rinaldi. "Got to keep him quiet for a few hours." This time he allowed Ivy to fill the syringe and plunge it into Texas's rump. Billy Joe watched, for once completely speechless.

Ivy helped Billy Joe make up an itchy, dirty

horse blanket bed for him to sleep in while he waited out a night vigil in the stable, watching Texas.

"In my truck's a thermos of hot soup for you, boy," said Dr. Rinaldi. "I guess this was the night for it." The doctor checked Texas over one more time. "He'll be okay, but he won't get up until morning. We'll send your dad out with the horse van at sunup," he added.

Ivy looked at Billy Joe. His face was not a picture of happiness.

"Don't tell my dad I was snake hunting, Ivy," whispered Billy Joe. "Swear to God?"

Ivy didn't answer. She didn't know what she would do. She just wanted to get home. It was past nine o'clock. Her mother would be waiting, watching at the window.

"Hop in the cab, Ivy. I'll give you a ride," said Dr. Rinaldi.

The warmed-up cab of Dr. Rinaldi's truck felt like a day in June to Ivy.

"Danged if I ever did see anything like that in my life," Dr. Rinaldi said. He lit his pipe and puffed on it. "That Billy Joe musta run into a rattler ball."

"Rattler ball?"

"Yup. Spooner Summit's got lots of rattlers. See, in summertime a west-facing mountain has a hundred flat-rock southern-sun exposures. Snakes love it. Then, in the winter they hibernate. Some go it alone, some wrap themselves up in balls of ten or twenty snakes. Makes your blood run cold! Somehow Billy Joe must have disturbed a rattler ball. How he could have done that is beyond me!"

Ivy decided not mention Billy Joe's ax, bag, and shovel to Dr. Rinaldi. She knew that birdbrained boy would already catch enough fire and brimstone in the morning.

"What time does Ruben get back from the old folks' home?" asked Dr. Rinaldi.

"He says he leaves when they serve up break-fast," answered Ivy. "He gets the first bus in the morning back to Spooner Lake."

"Good. That'll be just about the time Jim Butterworth drives up with the horse van to get Texas and his boy. Texas'll be back on his feet by that time; he's as tough as a bag of nails. When Ruben comes home," Dr. Rinaldi said dryly, "you can be sure he'll go over that filly of his for three hours, looking for nicks and scratches."

"I hope he doesn't find any!" said Ivy.

"I checked her before we left," said Dr. Rinaldi. "She's fine." He pulled again on his pipe. "Billy Joe is just trouble on two feet."

Ivy had no words for Billy Joe this time.

"You should be proud of yourself, Ivy," Dr. Rinaldi continued. "Not everybody can run a garden hose up a horse's snout. You've got nerves of steel. Think of this: Someday you'll run into a mare with a breech foal. You'll have to stick your whole arm in and pull her foal out of the womb or both'll die. Think you could do that, too?"

Ivy tried to picture it. "Well, if the mare was in pain, I guess I'd just have to do it," she said.

"Yup," agreed the doctor. "You do what you have to, even when it's the last thing you want to do. But on the other hand, when there's a little wet foal on the hay under his mother, and he stands up, it's like the world was made brand-new, right then and there."

It was at this moment in Dr. Rinaldi's pickup truck, with all its rattles and squeals, that quite out of nowhere, the emblem of the lamp in the hand came back to Ivy. Maybe it was the long, dark, cold night she'd just spent. Maybe it was the mention of a world made brand-new. Maybe it was both. Whatever triggered it, she remembered now where she had seen that emblem before. It was chiseled into the entrance gate of a Reno estate that she had passed many times in her father's pickup truck. The Mountain School. The Mountain School was a private prep school. The papers scattered in the back of Annie's car had been an application form for the following year.

"Oh . . . of course," Ivy found herself saying aloud.

"Come again?" asked Dr. Rinaldi.

"It's nothing, Dr. Rinaldi," said Ivy.

On Christmas morning, Ivy unwrapped her presents, all of them expected. There were the hand-knit sweaters, one from each of her grannies; a box of orange chocolates; and a new blouse and skirt made by her mother. Ivy had bought her mother a pair of cloud socks and her father a new set of leather work gloves from

Strunk's General Store. Hanging on the tree, however, was a package Ivy had not expected. It was from Annie.

"Someone put it in our mailbox," Ivy's mother said.

Inside the gold and red paper was a silver Tru-Friendship ring set with Ivy's birthstone, an amethyst. She turned it in her fingers. Annie must have received the tourmaline ring at camp after all. Ivy slipped the ring onto her finger and held out her hand so that the colored lights on the tree shone through the amethyst.

"Your dad and I miss seeing Annie around," said Ivy's mother. "Hope that ring means we'll be seeing her again."

"It's a good-bye present, Mom," Ivy said. "Annie's going to go to that private school her mom went to. The Mountain School."

"She tell you that?" asked her mother.

"No, but I know anyway," said Ivy.

"I guess public school's not good enough for those people," her mother said with a sniff. And this was true.

Ivy stood and roped her scarf around her neck. "I better rouse that Billy Joe and get on over the mountain to Andromeda," Ivy said.

"Hop in the truck, honey," said her dad.

"You driving me to the Montgomery place?" asked Ivy.

"Naw. You'll have to go tend your racehorse after noontime," said her dad. "Right now we gotta go to the airport. Somebody's coming in."

"But Billy Joe's dad always makes the airport run," said Ivy.

Her dad chuckled. "Jim Butterworth's out on their south hundred, honey, making sure Billy Joe don't slack off. Billy Joe's got two hundred fence posts to straighten and miles of bob wire to untangle."

"What happened, Dad?" Ivy asked as her

father pulled onto the highway north to Reno. She thought Billy Joe had gotten away with his rattler ball adventure.

"Well," he said, "at first Jim Butterworth just wrote off the whole snakebite business to bad luck: sleeping snake wakes up in the middle of winter. Snakes are snakes, and they'll bite your horse, never mind if you're a saint in heaven, even in the dead of winter."

Ivy waited for her dad to wind this story out. She was still not going to tell on Billy Joe. He was in enough trouble.

"Well, nothing more was made of it until last night," her dad continued. "Jim Butterworth had filled the wood bag with firewood, brought it into the house, and emptied it. Tumbling out after the firewood was a rattler head, neatly chopped off at the neck. Anyone who had the bad luck to brush a finger or two over one of those fangs, still full of venom, coulda been countin' sheep in heaven this very minute."

"Oh, Billy Joe," said Ivy.

"Yup," agreed her Dad. "Seems he was on purpose looking for hibernating rattler balls up there on Spooner Summit. Wanted to sell the skins to some boot maker in Reno. So he's got a winter of nasty outdoor work ahead. Cora says it'll learn him. I don't reckon anything'll learn that boy till he maybe blows a hand off with his danged fireworks. If they'd lost the horse, Billy Joe'd be strung up by his thumbs. But Texas is going to be okay."

Through the truck window, Ivy watched the bleached winter landscape fly by.

"What kind of guest is flying out here on Christmas Day, Dad?" asked Ivy.

But either her dad had no idea or he wasn't telling. Could it be a movie star from California?

Ivy wondered. No. Movie stars didn't stay at the Red Star Ranch, with its one little radiator in each cottage. They went to Reno or Las Vegas and relaxed at the big ranches with heated indoor pools and people who gave you massages.

Ivy and her dad could hear the eleven o'clock plane a ways off in the sky. Because of the short landing strip, flights into Reno had to circle like paper airplanes in a stairwell.

They pulled up to the tarmac, got out of the truck, and watched the plane land.

Ivy looked at the travelers' faces one by one as they emerged into the bright Nevada sunshine. Her dad didn't flag anyone and no one stopped.

"Where's the Red Star Ranch sign, Dad?" Ivy asked. "Shouldn't we be holding it up so the person knows who we are?"

"Don't need one," said her father mysteriously.

"Why? Who's coming?" asked Ivy again.

"Here he is!" said Ivy's dad.

Ivy recognized the man immediately. She didn't think she'd ever forget his crew cut and the American Airlines uniform. He was holding a leash. At the end of the leash was a much bigger shepherd than she remembered, the tip of one ear gone now. Inca knew her at once.

★ ★ ★

Late Christmas afternoon, Ivy decided she'd pay Billy Joe a visit in the south pasture, where he was deep in drifts of snow.

"Billy Joe!" Ivy called. He saw her. A big smile lit up his face.

"What are you doing here?" he asked.

"I was in my living room, where it was nice and warm," she explained. "I thought of you out here, with your fingers freezing off. So I figured, no matter what stupid thing you'd done, I should bring you a thermos of cocoa."

Billy Joe stood up from the hole he was clearing out, brushed the snow off his jacket, and reached for the thermos as if it were the Holy Grail itself.

"Who's that dog?" he asked.

"It's Inca!" said Ivy.

And before Billy Joe could react, the dog pushed him over into the snow and kissed him. Billy Joe laughed.

Ivy poured hot chocolate into the thermos cup and gave it to Billy Joe. "What happened to his ear?" he asked.

"Mr. Burgess says he got into fights with Siegfried and Tristan," Ivy explained. "They nearly killed him. So Mr. Burgess decided to send him back to me. He arrived on the eleven o'clock flight just this morning, with a year's worth of dog food right in the baggage compartment."

Inca leaned against Ivy. Her fingers found his bitten-off velvet ear. Inca was twenty pounds heavier than when he'd left, but he had forgotten nothing. In his eyes Ivy could see that she was his "one" for all time.

Billy Joe took a slug of the hot chocolate.

"You'd better come in, Billy Joe," Ivy said. "It's getting dark."

The two walked home with Inca dancing and prancing between them.

"This afternoon, I got a telephone call," Ivy told Billy Joe. "Somebody's ranch man down in Sandstone Canyon broke an ankle. Three paddock horses. Ice breaking, water carrying, three flakes a day. You wanna help out when you're finished here?"

"You're kidding, right?" said Billy Joe. "I'm nothing but trouble."

"I'll watch you like a hawk," Ivy said.

"Fifty-fifty?" he asked.

"No snakes, no firecrackers, and no trouble," said Ivy.

"Deal!" said Billy Joe. He held out his dirty work glove, full of icy holes and fence post splinters.

Ivy slapped it. "Deal," she said.

The author in Nevada, 1958